Suffer the Little Ones

Suffer the Little Ones

by
James H. Ryan

Aurora Publishers Incorporated
NASHVILLE/LONDON

813.54
R95s
81715
2 an. 1973

Dedication

To Joyce, and of course, to Kathy, Thom, and Peachy—the keepers of the secret.

And to the memory of Max Siegel. He was a great literary agent and friend to the neophyte.

Your children are not your children.

They are the sons and daughters of Life's longing for itself.

They come through you but not from you,

And though they are with you, yet they belong not to you.

You may give them your love but not your thoughts.

For they have their own thoughts.

You may house their bodies but not their souls,

For their souls dwell in the house of tomorrow, which you cannot visit, not even in your dreams.

You may strive to be like them, but seek not to make them like you.

For life goes not backward nor tarries with yesterday. . . .

Author's Note

The prevention and treatment of childhood ailments—be they congenital, acquired, infectious, neoplastic, or traumatic—have made great strides within the past several years. Within this steady, if tardy progress, a faint shade, soon recognized to be a blotch, then a growing malignancy, began to emerge. This is the curse of child abuse.

It is not a simple thing, this overt or covert mistreatment of our offspring. Rather, it's a hideous and insidious mixture of expectation, frustration, negligence, and appalling violence—to the point that survival itself becomes the basic issue.

You react to this illogical abortion of what a child's world should be. It makes you sick. Then mad. And then confused. You end up face-to-face with the why of it all. Why must the little ones suffer?

And what do you do about it? How do you treat the universally innocent victims? The abusers? Above all, how do you prevent further child negligence, battering, and murder?

The key to prevention is understanding. And that's what this is all about.

James H. Ryan

Contents

CHAPTER I

"Ladies and gentlemen, Captain Brown has turned off the seatbelt light. Please feel free to move about the cabin if you desire. For your added protection, in case of any sudden turbulence, may I suggest that you keep your seatbelt fastened when you are in your seats. Thank you."

Dr. Brennan loosened his seatbelt and took his briefcase from under the seat. He placed the mediocre paperback mystery he'd bought at the airport inside and extracted a substantial bundle of papers. He planned to use his flight time to proofread the galleys of the second edition of his book on child abuse.

He stared at the words on the rough paper, but he could not force himself to concentrate. All he could think of was the naked girl. Something he'd forgotten was bothering him.

"Pardon."

Brennan reluctantly directed his attention to the fat man sitting to his left. "Yes?"

"You an author?" Pointing a pudgy finger at the galleys, he persisted. "Is that a book you're writing?"

"Yes," Brennan replied unenthusiastically.

"Well, I'll be damned. Imagine me sitting next to a real author—shows you it pays to go first class. I'm Fred Coleman, Kansas City."

"Patrick Brennan, St. Louis." He intentionally avoided his professional title. The word doctor all too often precipitated a boring session of listening to the many complaints of some

1

good soul intent on obtaining an exhaustive verbal consultation.

Just at this moment the stewardess handed him a small tray with two miniature bottles of scotch. "You wanted ice, Dr. Brennan?"

"Yes, thank you," he answered as he shifted the galleys to make room for his drink. That blows my cover, he thought. He sincerely hoped his travelling companion was in perfect health.

"You a medical man?" Coleman asked. "M.D.?"

"Yes, a pediatrician."

"What's your book about?"

"It's about child abuse, Mr. Coleman," Brennan said coolly.

"Oh." Coleman glanced down the aisle, attracted the attention of a pretty hostess, and asked for a newspaper. She brought him the Sunday edition of the **Chicago Tribune,** and he was soon busy thumbing through the bulk of the paper.

Brennan sipped his drink. He looked at the galleys, but he couldn't keep his mind on them. He kept envisioning the naked girl. No, he remembered now that she hadn't been entirely naked. There was a narrow plastic identification band stapled around her ankle. But aside from that, she was wearing her birthday suit. Appropriate, Brennan mused, since this was the day she was born.

What the hell was it he'd forgotten? He knew he wouldn't get anything else done until he remembered it. God, with all the hectic last minute chores he'd had to do before he could leave his practice for just a few days, it was a wonder he hadn't forgotten his name. Still, that was no excuse. If he was to fulfill his professional obligation to this baby—what was her name? Webster, that was it—he had to remember.

Brennan decided to review the whole physical examination. Maybe that would trigger a recollection. The doctor envisioned the scene in the newborn nursery that morning. The general appearance of the Webster baby was normal. He remembered guiding the small stethescope over her heart and lungs. Breath and heart beat were normal. He'd examined her abdomen next. Nothing wrong there. The cut section of the umbilical cord revealed the stumps of two arteries and a single vein. A solitary artery, an anomaly occasionally associated with serious birth defects, would immediately have attracted his attention.

External genitalia were okay. When he'd placed his palm flat against the sole of her foot, it had exerted the familiar pressure of the stretch reflex. Similarly, when he put his palm to her face in imitation of her mother's breast, she'd made sucking motions with her lips and moved her mouth toward his hand. "That's a good rooting reflex, Miss," Brennan had commented. "Nice to see you know what your mouth is for."

Brennan realized his habit of carrying on a one-sided conversation with newborns often elicited wide-eyed and somewhat skeptical reactions from the students in the nursery. But the old pros, like Miss Bentley, the head nurse, scarcely noticed this idiosyncrasy.

Bentley was a maiden lady of indeterminate age, somewhere over fifty. She was a rather plump and even-tempered nurse of the old school, who expertly assisted the newborns through this most dangerous period of transition from the intrauterine dependence of fetal life to the independence of the air-breathing neonate. Miss Bentley's world consisted of "her" babies, the doctors and other hospital workers, and her daily pilgrimage to Saint Mary's Church for six A.M. mass.

The mental search continued. Fontanelle okay, mouth normal, palate intact. Her eyes were bright and her facial expression relaxed, not the worried one that frequently was the hallmark of a sick infant. Tonic neck and mass startle reflexes okay. Her backside was completely normal.

Little Miss Webster had begun to rebel against all this bothersome probing with a few whimpering cries. Her protest became a lusty wailing when he inserted a thermometer into her rectum.

Then Brennan remembered he'd checked her hips. "That's it," he said aloud.

"What?" Coleman fumbled with his newspaper.

"Nothing, Mr. Coleman," Brennan reassured him. Slightly embarrassed, he shifted his mind back to the nursery. The Webster baby's left hip had been a little tight. He couldn't get total abduction on that side, while the right thigh readily depressed all the way to the surface of the examination table.

The doctor remembered it was just at that moment that Miss Bentley had interrupted him with a lab report on the jaundiced baby they were treating with phototherapy. The bilirubin, or level of jaundice pigment in the blood, had dropped significantly. Brennan had told her to turn off the bright light over the baby's crib, remove the blindfold that shielded his eyes from the intense illumination, and dress him. The little guy had responded beautifully, so now the phototherapy could safely be discontinued. Neither Brennan nor his professional colleagues knew exactly why, but total body exposure to bright white light speeded up the removal of the potentially brain damaging bilirubin from the newborn.

The distraction had almost caused Brennan to commit a grave error. Now that he remembered, he wrote a note on the front page of his galleys: Webster baby—x-ray hips. It wasn't too urgent; it could safely wait until his return to St. Louis next week. The x-ray would tell him if her left hip joint was too shallow. If it was, he'd refer her to an orthopedist for treatment. Otherwise the condition could progress to a dislocated hip and a short leg—a future Miss Webster would no doubt find highly undesirable.

This worry removed from his mind, Brennan turned his attention back to the galleys. He found his place, and tried again to resume his reading. After a futile attempt to concentrate, he set aside his pen, opened the second bottle of scotch, and

4

poured it over the dwindling supply of ice in his glass. He just couldn't read the galleys now. His editor would understand, Brennan rationalized. She had always been very patient with him.

Overworked—I'm getting paranoid, Brennan thought. But it was all too true. Things seemed to have been much too hectic lately. He sipped his drink, stretched his long legs as best he could within the confines of the seat, and sighed deeply.

Sighing respiration is a symptom of neurosis, Brennan reminded himself. So what, he thought. Show me a pediatrician who hasn't personally experienced most of the complaints of the neurotic, and I'll show you one of those professorial types, safely enshrouded in the higher echelons of a medical school and protected by phalanxes of eager underlings from the perennial trials and tribulations of delivering health care in the marketplace.

This brought to mind one of his pet peeves. When politicians and other concerned groups addressed themselves to the problems of health care in the nation, they invariably picked a group of these medical bureaucrats to seek the solutions. The problems were very real, Brennan readily admitted. But these doctors who could schedule their every move, who couldn't remember the last time a jangling telephone had robbed them of sleep—somehow they seemed out of place proclaiming their high-sounding theories on how to get the medically deprived the care and treatment they needed and deserved.

Oh well, at least in one problem area a front-line practitioner—Dr. Patrick Brennan, to be specific—would soon have his day in the forum. He'd spent Saturday afternoon closeted with Mark Gray, the eager legislative assistant to Senator Hiram Black of Michigan. Senator Black was the chairman of the powerful Senate Committee on Health, Education and Welfare. As a result of this conference, Brennan would testify before the full committee in a few weeks. That should cause an epidemic of headaches among various fat cats in the Food and Drug Administration, and, hopefully, it would compel the Gastropep people to get that damn salol out of their product.

Brennan resumed his aimless thumbing through the galleys. It was useless effort, but at least it restrained the vociferous Mr. Coleman. He'd noted the obese gentleman casting hopeful glances at him periodically. Brennan just didn't feel up to a lot of aimless talking. Actually, he felt like sleeping for a week. In a room without a phone. In a place with no parents and no children.

Patrick Brennan could scarcely remember a time in his forty-plus years when he had not been chronically tired. He'd had a reasonable childhood. But since starting med school, it seemed he'd been on a treadmill that kept going faster and faster. Lately, except for an occasional vacation, he seemed to have been getting himself more and more involved in an ever-increasing number of medical and paramedical endeavors. Many in the latter category—serving on various committees, that sort of thing—pointed up glaring social needs in his community, but rarely led to workable solutions. Frustrating.

Brennan realized he had to go to the john. He released his seat-belt and excused himself as he awkwardly eased past Fred Coleman.

On his way, he handed his glass and two empty liquor vials to the hostess. She asked if he wanted another drink and muttered her thanks after Brennan's polite refusal. Nice-looking guy, she thought. Graying hair makes him look distinguished. Takes care of himself too, she guessed. Probably married and has six kids. Too old for me anyway, she thought as she deposited the empties in the trash drawer.

Her assumption about Dr. Brennan's marital status was wrong. He was and always had been single. And he was considered very eligible by a number of St. Louis women—including several as young as the pretty hostess.

Upon his return a few minutes later, Brennan knew by Mr. Coleman's eager expression that he had lost his chance for further solitude. His suspicion was immediately confirmed. "Look at this," Coleman said, pointing to a small article in the newspaper. "Sounds like it's right down your alley, Doc."

The article was headlined, "Mother's Murder Trial To Begin." It was datelined Rossdale, Illinois, January 23. Brennan read that the trial of Jacqueline Teal, accused slayer of her two-year-old daughter, Helen, was to begin the following day in Rossdale. The murder had taken place last September. Mrs. Teal had been confined in the Ross County Jail since her arrest on the day of the slaying. According to State's Attorney Harold Keller, the state would show that Mrs. Teal had physically abused her infant daughter for months prior to the actual killing.

"Terrible thing, isn't it, Doc," Coleman said. "That what your book is about?"

"Yes."

"A woman would have to be crazy to do that to her own flesh and blood," Coleman continued. "And premeditated too. Says so right there in the paper. Beat that poor kid for months, she did. Makes you sick, don't it?"

"Yes, it makes me sick," Brennan replied quietly.

"Wouldn't expect that sort of thing in a little town like Rossdale. I've driven through there. Quiet little place. Several thousand people. Probably a nice place to live. None of the problems of a big city. No sir, wouldn't expect a monster like that mother to show up in a place like Rossdale. But you just never know."

Brennan began leafing through his galleys again, hoping his obvious disinterest would prevail. This was not to be. Coleman leaned toward him and said, "As a baby doctor, I guess you'd like to see that Teal bitch hang. Right, Doc?"

7

"It isn't all that simple," Brennan replied.

"What else can they do? Who ever heard of a mother killing her own kid? Why, that's not natural."

"Is murder ever natural, Mr. Coleman?"

"Call me Fred. I don't know—some people deserve killin'. But not a two-year-old kid. And not by her mother. Hope the judge is a family man. Then he'll know what to do to that worthless whore."

Christ, Brennan thought, this guy's ready to bring out the stake and light her up. The virulent Mr. Coleman reminded him of a medical colleague who, after the fatal shooting of antiwar protesters a couple of years before, had recommended killing a few hundred more longhairs just to get their attention.

The Fasten Seat Belt sign flicked on. Brennan obeyed it. He picked up his briefcase, put his neglected galleys inside, and settled back for the landing at O'Hare airport.

"You sure didn't have much to say about that murder," Coleman whined. "Thought you'd be interested in it."

Brennan looked at Coleman for several seconds, then said quietly, yet precisely, "Mr. Coleman, I'm on my way to Rossdale. I'm to be an expert witness in this Teal case. I therefore think it inappropriate for me to discuss this particular case, even under unofficial circumstances.

"I will say this, however, Mr. Coleman. Most people are repelled by the thought of a parent attacking his child. I am too. I don't like the fact that child abuse exists any more than you do. But I don't like cancer either. Both adversely affect the health of my patients. And I feel I owe it to my profession and to my patients to try and understand this child abuse problem, so I can prevent and treat it just like any other disorder. And that, sir, is the extent of my interest in the whole miserable subject."

The jet engines revved down to a whisper and the No Smoking sign flashed on.

CHAPTER II

Just on the outskirts of Rossdale, Dr. Brennan spotted the motel. It looked nice enough—two-story brick and frame construction, surrounded by carefully tended grounds. Brennan flipped the turn signal on the rental car, hesitated, then decided that since it was still early, he would take a quick and unescorted tour of the town before settling into his lodgings.

As he drove about, he decided that Rossdale was probably a nice little city, but that this January afternoon was just not the best time for touring. The midwinter grays and ochers and umbers did little to emphasize the quiet beauty of the small midwestern municipality. Oaks and doomed but surviving elms interlaced their skeletal fingers high above the streets. The houses were neat—some old, some new. There were no patterned, look-alike neighborhoods. Rather, Rossdale exhibited the kind of architectural randomness that characterizes the midsection of the country.

In the downtown area, a group of stores and shops spread out in all directions from the railroad tracks that pierced the heart of the place like an arrow. The three-story granite courthouse sat like a contented Buddha amidst the artifacts that surrounded it—a union soldier, musket at the ready, frozen in greenish bronze; a field piece of World War I vintage; and finally, a polished marble monolith engraved with the names of the dead heroes of the second global conflict. It seemed to Brennan that they were written in very small print.

9

This place of justice was the physician's immediate goal here in Rossdale. But not now. Tomorrow.

After the ten o'clock news, Brennan took a quick shower and climbed into bed. His bedtime ritual further required that he read something. At home he frequently scanned one or another of the deluge of minor medical journals that every day's mail seemed to bring. Tonight, since he was too exhausted to devote any time to his galleys, he had to be satisfied with the small brochure he'd picked up in the motel lobby.

The folder was entitled "Welcome to Rossdale," and clearly stated, "This Colorful Pamphlet Provided Free By The Rossdale Chamber of Commerce." On the front was a picture of the bronze Union soldier Brennan had seen standing on the courthouse lawn.

The first white men thought to have visited what is now Ross County were the French-Canadian fur traders, the text began. Upon their arrival in the latter half of the eighteenth century, these lusty explorers found the rolling hill country inhabited by the Indians of the Foxes tribe, as well as by the belligerent Sac of the Rock River. Who wouldn't be belligerent, Brennan thought, with all those Canucks screwing your people, materially and physically.

The area was opened to white settlers by treaty with the Indians early in the nineteenth century, he read. Finally got the job done on the aborigines, he mused.

The city and county were named for a pioneer named Ninian Ross. Anyone, Brennan reasoned, who had to go through life with a name like Ninian deserved to be immortalized.

Scandinavian immigrants provided the major ethnic background for the farmers and early townsmen. With the coming of the railroad in the 1850's, large numbers of Irish and Welsh moved in. As the years passed, representatives of many other nationalities made their homes in Rossdale.

Rossdale had changed a great deal in the last quarter of a

century. Numerous manufacturing plants had located in what had previously been a farming and dairy center. The city's population increased steadily during this period. Rossdale now boasted a population in excess of 18,000.

Rossdale was the proud owner of a brand new junior college, and its public and parochial school systems were second to none in the area. Probably rapidly going broke like most of the others in the country, Brennan imagined. But the Chamber of Commerce could hardly put that in their promotional literature.

All the major churches and a temple were to be found in Rossdale. A modern 120-bed community hospital served the health needs of the citizenry. Now, that's getting down to the meat of the propaganda as far as I'm concerned, Brennan thought. He was more impressed by the photographs of the hospital than he had been by anything else in the brochure. He smiled at his own bias, clicked off the light, and soon fell asleep.

Patrick Brennan parked his automobile behind the courthouse, opposite the spaces reserved for county officials. He noted that a not very new Cadillac was already parked in the slot marked Judge Pieter Waggoner. The judge was obviously a man who believed in getting to work on time. Shrewd deduction, Brennan thought. Good way to start playing the high-powered medical investigator. Or medical witness. Or whatever he was supposed to be in this Teal case.

Brennan surveyed the marble interior of the building. There was a great central courtyard that extended upward through all three stories of the building and culminated in a concave panorama of the huge domed roof. The elevator and building directory were located on the far side of the courtyard. He strode rapidly across the polished marble floor, glanced at the building directory and stepped into the elevator.

Brennan located room 300, peered at the brass plate on the door to make sure he had the right office, and walked inside. He was greeted by a middle-aged secretary who promptly and graciously showed him into Judge Waggoner's office.

The judge stood before a large window, his back to the door. He seemed to be either deep in thought or very absorbed in the scene below. Brennan noted that the judge was slim and exceptionally tall. Then, as the gentleman turned, Brennan saw that he looked like a beardless Lincoln with gray unruly hair. Just perfect.

"Dr. Brennan?"

"Yes."

"Come in. Come in." The judge crossed the room in two strides and enthusiastically shook the physician's hand. "Sit down. Make yourself comfortable, Doctor."

Brennan sat down in a comfortably worn leather armchair and looked around the room. It was all masculine—rich paneling, shelves of books, massive furnishings. A serious, but pleasant and comfortable room.

"Welcome to Rossdale, Doctor" said the judge as he sat down at his desk. He leaned forward and a stray lock of hair shifted down over his pale forehead. "And that, Dr. Brennan, just might be the last welcome you're going to get here. When the people of my fair city learn you're to investigate the Teal case, they won't exactly welcome you with open arms."

"Sounds ominous."

"It is. Small town hysteria. Lucky the defense asked for a bench trial. It would've been impossible to impanel an impartial jury unless we'd had a change in venue." He paused and leaned back in his chair. "I'd be off the hook now if that had happened. But it didn't, so I'm still stuck with the mess, Doctor, and I'm about to drag you into the muck right along with me."

"May I ask in just what specific capacity I'm to become befouled?" Brennan queried.

12

"Well, sir, I'll tell you a secret." The judge picked up a partially consumed pipe, gently tapped the ash off the top of the tobacco, and began groping about for a match. In due time he got the pipe going to his satisfaction. He leaned forward into the haze of aromatic smoke and continued. "Sorry I couldn't tell you before now. You'll understand why shortly."

He sat back in his swivel chair, folded his hands across his lean midsection, and contemplated the physician for a moment longer. "In a minute I'm going to have to go out that door and through another door into my courtroom. I'm going to sit at that high bench and open the trial of the People of the State of Illinois versus Mrs. Jacqueline Teal. And I'm going to sit up there and listen as a young lawyer, named Delaney, politely enters a change of plea. He will acknowledge that his client, Mrs. Teal, is guilty to the charge of murder in regard to the death of her child, Helen."

"Guilty! Really? Well, I'll be damned." Patrick Brennan was surprised. He was also confused. He had assumed that he had once again been called as an expert medical witness with a degree of experience in the distasteful subject of child abuse. Apparently he had been mistaken. Why then, Brennan wondered, had he been called to Rossdale?

"Don't look so puzzled, Doctor. I'll explain everything to you. Now where was I? A plea of guilty. Delaney tried to make a deal with Harold Keller, the state's attorney. He wanted Keller to settle for a reduced plea—voluntary manslaughter. Well, old Harold didn't buy it. He's usually willing to deal for a lesser charge, but public opinion is running high in this Teal case—and Harold wants to run again. Manslaughter's just not a strong enough charge to suit the folks here. Of course, Harold won't hold out for the death penalty. He did give a little.

"Now, I'll tell you where you fit into all this, Dr. Brennan. In the preliminaries of this case, we had a sanity hearing for the defendant. Three qualified psychiatrists attested individual-

13

ly and collectively to the fact that Mrs. Teal was sane—in the legal sense of the word.

"And now comes this guilty plea, which I will have to accept." Again the judge swung back in his swivel chair. He stared at the old-fashioned high ceiling. Then he quietly and soberly added, "And then I'll have to come up with an appropriate sentence for the guilty murderess."

"I don't envy you, Judge."

"I know, Doctor, I know. It's always been hard for me to hand out the penalties. Once, years ago, I had to—Oh well, that's another story. At any rate, Dr. Brennan, I don't want your envy. I want your help."

"Judge Waggoner, I came here for a couple of reasons. At least one of them was simply to get out of St. Louis for a brief respite from some professional problems. However, to borrow your phrase, that's another story. But mostly I came to help. Now just who I was to try and help, I didn't quite know. Thinking back on it, I should have known this was all a little different from the usual expert testimony request. How often does the initial contact emanate from the judge in an abused child case? It has always been the defense or the prosecution who requested my humble opinions—at least in the criminal courts. I guess I was just too preoccupied for this subtle difference to register."

Brennan paused to light a cigarette, inhaled deeply, then continued, "At any rate, Judge, I came to help. I have the greater part of a week free before I have to return to St. Louis. So what can I do?"

Pieter Waggoner leaned forward, elbows on the desk, hands clasped. Staring directly at Brennan, he said quietly and distinctly, "That's up to you, Doctor. I'm giving you a blank check."

"What?" Brennan involuntarily reacted to this unforeseen offer.

"Carte blanche. Blank check. Free hand. Autonomy. That's

14

what I'm willing to give you. Within the limits of the law, of course."

"Why?"

"Do you know what an amicus curiae is?"

"A friend of the court."

"Right. In your instance, an expert witness who is in no way a party to the litigation. One who is invited by the court to give advice upon some matter pending before it. This particular matter involves a young mother, a murdered infant, and a judge who must attempt to resolve the many dilemmas that this simple-sounding equation ultimately postulates. Do you understand what I'm up against? What I'm trying to say?"

"I think I do, Judge."

"I need help, Dr. Brennan. I need it desperately. No. Just a minute. I don't want to give you the wrong idea." The tall jurist was very intent. With that wondrous semantic agility inbred in every good barrister, he had immediately recognized a potential misconception and now sought to correct it. "I'm not trying to evade my responsibility in this case. I'm not attempting to saddle you with my job—or anyone else, for that matter. But this is an unusual situation, and I'm asking for counsel from a recognized authority in a very specialized field. Understand?"

"I think so."

"Good. Now we have to lay some ground rules. Are you acquainted with the M'Naughten Decision?"

"To a limited extent."

"Well, just so you and I both know where we are and, hopefully, where we're going, I'm going to give you a quick review. Now, about the middle of the last century the prime minister of England was Sir Robert Peel. Very able man, so they say. Like our contemporary statesmen, Sir Robert lived in a time when there was an open season on political personalities. He had no difficulty in acquiring a number of enemies, and one of these was a crackpot named M'Naughten. This gentleman decided to assassinate Mr. Peel, thinking him to be the source of countless evils. But it seems his homicide was as confused as he was. He mistakenly shot one Mr. Drummond who had the fatal misfortune of being Peel's secretary. M'Naughten was eventually found not guilty on the grounds of insanity.

"The essence of the so-called M'Naughten Rule, as it comes down to us, is that the accused must know the difference between right and wrong in order to be held liable under the law. In Illinois the accused must also be able to cooperate with a defense attorney in order to stand trial.

"Now a couple of more recent decisions have slightly modified the legal approach to the question of sanity. The Durham Decision states that an accused is not criminally responsible if his unlawful act was the result of mental disease or mental defect. This rule was laid down in 1954. That isn't much of an advance in the legal recognition of the liability of the mentally disturbed in 111 years, but I suppose every little bit helps.

"Then we have yet a more recent ruling, the Currens Decision. Here the offender is excused if he acts as a consequence of mental defect or disease, and if he, at the time of the act, lacks the capacity to resist the commission of the crime. They call this diminished capacity. This defense was recently put forward in the trial of Sirhan Sirhan, the man who murdered Senator Kennedy. The California jury rejected it in that case, you'll recall.

"Have I made everything clear?"

"Perfectly clear, Judge."

"Well, for our purposes, the psychiatrists who examined Mrs. Teal applied all these criteria. And they unanimously agreed that the woman is sane. Legally sane. This means she is responsible for her actions. She is accountable to society for the murder of her daughter, Helen. Understand?"

"Yes."

"Do you agree? Do you think a mother who could and in fact did murder her infant daughter is sane?"

"Judge, please. Medical sanity is not the same as legal sanity. It just isn't that cut and dried from the medical standpoint. The therapeutic definition of diminished mental capacity lacks the didactic all-or-nothing concept of the legal definition."

"I'm not asking you for a comparative analysis of the various definitions of sanity, Doctor. I want your opinion. Do you or do you not think that Mrs. Teal is sane?"

The judge continued to stare at Brennan. The physician did not seem disturbed by his host's abrupt change in tone.

"I can't answer that question," Brennan began. "I'm no psychiatrist. I haven't even seen the woman, much less examined her. And unless she is a raving lunatic, I would not consider myself qualified to give you a worthwhile or usable opinion as to her mental status."

The judge stood up, came around the desk, and extended his hand. "Congratulations. You just passed my test with flying colors, Dr. Brennan. No preformed idea that only a mad woman would beat her child to death. No trying to be a lawyer like so many other physicians who have appeared in my court. By God, I think maybe I chose the right man for the job this time!"

"Thank you, Your Honor. I hope you're right," Brennan replied. He was more ill at ease now than he had been earlier, during the judge's interrogation.

The judge had to go into his courtroom, but there were details yet that required their attention. The "blank check" was presented to the physician in the form of a formal court order that required any and all principals involved in the matter of the State versus Mrs. Teal to cooperate completely with Patrick Brennan, M.D., amicus curiae of Associate Circuit Judge Pieter Waggoner.

"Any facet of the investigation, any officer of the court,

any witness, any evidence, the defendant—anything your heart desires—is open to you."

The judge continued hurriedly, yet with conviction, "To do my job, I need to try to understand why a parent—a parent who has been declared legally sane—would abuse a child to the point of death. A single act of intense passion resulting in homicide I can readily understand. The same with violent death inflicted by a psychotic, or sadistic, or psychopathic personality. But this Teal case really doesn't fit any of the categories with which I'm familiar.

"That's why you're here, Dr. Brennan—to help me comprehend." Judge Waggonner looked at his watch and stood up. "I have to go into the courtroom now and accept that plea. We both have a busy day ahead, Doctor, so we'd better get started."

As Judge Waggoner donned the long black robe of his office, he hesitated once more. "I'll recess the trial this morning and set a hearing for aggravation and mitigation for ten o'clock on Friday. That give you enough time?"

"What kind of hearing for Friday? I'm afraid I don't quite understand."

"Sort of a finale, before I sentence Mrs. Teal," the judge said as he zipped up his gown. "All Mrs. Teal will have said up to this point is 'I'm guilty.' No judge or jury will have officially reiewed the corpus delicti, or any of the facts of the crime. Consequently, the state will argue the aggravation aspects of the case Friday—those things that increase the seriousness of this particular act of murder.

"The defense presents the other side, the mitigating circumstances. What is there in Mrs. Teal's act, or background, or what-have-you that should influence the judge to lessen the severity of the penalty."

"Is this an adversary hearing?" Brennan interrupted.

"Only partially. If it's to be meaningful, I'll have to allow a little more latitude. It's not a trial. The guilty plea takes

18

care of that. It's a matter of arguing the degree of guilt the judge should consider. And this would be difficult if strict trial rules were followed. Understand?"

"Yes, Judge. Should make my job a lot more meaningful."

"Exactly," Waggoner agreed. "See you Friday." The ebony-clad jurist shook Brennan's hand and hurried out the door.

As Brennan was leaving the judge's office, he paused in front of a sign that read, Harold J. Keller, State's Attorney. He thought he might as well attempt to see this county official while he was there. Keller's receptionist, a tall, slender blond informed him that Mr. Keller was in court at the moment. If the doctor would like to wait, she was confident Mr. Keller would soon be at his disposal.

The prospect of admiring her seemed more attractive to Brennan than anything else he had to do at the moment, so he sat down in one of the wooden chairs. He picked up a tattered copy of **Life,** intending to use it as a prop, but before he could get settled, a highly nervous man came hurrying through the doorway. He was holding a legal-size, bulging, brown file. "Oh, my God, where's Friday's court calendar? Judge Waggoner just set the Teal hearing for Friday. Have to cancel everything. No concern at all for others. No professional courtesy around here at all. Oh, my God."

"The calendar is still on your desk, Mr. Keller," the Valkyrie answered with exaggerated patience. "And this gentleman, Dr. Brennan, is waiting to see you."

Harold Keller whirled about and advanced to meet his guest. After a terse handshake he asked, "What can I do for you, Doctor?"

"Well, I —"

"Oh, you're the child beating expert," Keller interrupted. "You're that doctor. What's the name again? Brennan?"

"Don't know if I'd put it quite that way, Mr. Keller,"

Brennan said with a friendly smile. "And the name is Patrick Brennan."

"Put it that way? Oh yes, ha ha. See what you mean. Sorry." He darted off down an inner hallway, muttering, "Come along, come along." Brennan shrugged his shoulders at Keller's lovely if somewhat irritable receptionist and reluctantly followed his host.

"Sit right there, Doctor. Now, what can I do for you? Where do you want to begin?"

"You know I'm belatedly involved in this child-murder case?" Brennan asked.

"Yes. Hope you can help us. Don't see how, really, but I'll try to help. I always cooperate. No one else around here does."

Keller's voice was just a little above medium pitch and he seemed to be perpetually nervous. He reminded Brennan of a mother hen, though he was not at all effeminate. Actually, he wasn't a bad looking guy. Brennan estimated Keller to be a few years older than himself. Not as tall. Rather careless in his dress. His suit collar was turned up in back, and his tie, obviously not purchased with a shirt of this color in mind, was slightly askew.

"You're welcome to see the records, of course. The judge's order covers that. Copies too, if you like." Keller thrust the file he was still carrying toward his guest. "Here, take it," he offered. Before Brennan could do so, Keller added, "Oh, I'd better look at the judge's order first. Not that I don't think you're the right doctor. Got to be legal about these things, you know."

Brennan pulled the court order from his pocket, and handed it to Keller, who fluttered through the pages for an instant, then returned them. "All quite proper," he said.

"What's in the file that might help me, Mr. Keller?" Brennan didn't relish the prospect of wading through every single page in the bulging file.

"Oh, witness lists, transcripts of the preliminary hearings,

20

stuff like that. We were all ready to go to trial on this, you know. Ready and willing. Would have insisted on the death penalty. Really intended to. That's sort of silly anymore. Haven't had an execution in this state in years. And I can't even remember the last woman who was electrocuted."

"How about the sanity hearings?" Brennan asked. "I understand Mrs.—what's her name? Teal. I'd naturally be particularly interested in the opinions of the psychiatrists."

"Sure, sure. I already have a complete copy for you. You want police reports, stuff like that?"

"Maybe. At the moment, I think I'd rather hit that aspect of it firsthand. You know, the direct approach. Get personal impressions instead of reports."

"Very good, Doctor," Mr. Keller agreed vigorously. "Proper reasoning. Impressions, in a role like yours, are definitely the thing."

"Speaking of impressions, Mr. Keller. What do you think of the case?"

"Jacqueline Teal is definitely guilty of premeditated murder. No doubt about it," he answered. "If we went to trial, I'd win. Even get the death penalty. That doesn't mean she would actually die. Probably wouldn't. So, in the interest of time, and to save the taxpayers' money, I thought it best to accept Delaney's offer. He's her lawyer, you know."

"Yes. And that's another thing. Why a Chicago lawyer?"

"We have no public defender here, Dr. Brennan. County's too small. Don't need one."

Brennan wondered why, if the people could afford a full-time prosecutor, they could not, in this day and age, employ an equally compensated public defender.

"The judge appoints an attorney for people like Mrs. Teal," Harold rather disparagingly remarked. "But in this case, because of a considerable amount of coverage by the news media, particularly in Chicago, the A.C.L.U. volunteered a lawyer for her. Mr. Delaney.

"Believe you me," the state's attorney confided with a chuckle, "the local attorneys were damn happy to get off the hook."

"May I ask you a very candid question, Mr. Keller?"

"Of course, Dr. Brennan."

"What do you think of my being called into the case?"

"What do I think about your role?" Keller repeated. "To be brief, Doctor, you're wasting your time here."

"Why, Mr. Keller?"

"I hate to sound trite, but this case is open and shut. It's that simple. So what can you accomplish? She pleaded guilty. She'll go to prison, for the rest of her life if I have anything to say about it. And society will be considerably better off with her locked away. All this will happen, Doctor, with or without your presence in Rossdale. So, frankly, I can't see how you can possibly change any of this. Therefore, I think you're wasting your time."

"That's candid, all right."

"I'm a very direct person, Dr. Brennan. You asked, I answered." Softer then, with a note of kindness in his voice, Keller added, "I hope I haven't offended you."

"Not at all."

"Frankly, Dr. Brennan—and confidentially, if I might speak off the record for a moment."

"Of course."

"I'm a little worried about Judge Waggoner. Oh, don't misunderstand. I'm not doubting his mental competence. Not at all. But he is getting rather old, you know."

"He seemed pretty sharp to me," Brennan interjected.

"Well, I'm not even remotely suggesting senility. I mean— how should I say it?" Keller paused to think out his phraseology. "Maybe felony court is too much for Pieter anymore. Maybe Judge Waggoner is just losing his nerve."

CHAPTER III

Patrick Brennan sat alone in the Rossdale City Police Station and waited for the arrival of Captain Miller, who was already fifteen minutes late. He looked around in vain for something to read, then lit a cigarette.

He realized he was tormenting his cardiovascular system and respiratory tract, as well as polluting the air, but he really didn't care. A death wish? Hardly. Slow suicide? Probably. But he had long ago accepted the fact that his remaining vices were very precious to him. He enjoyed a drink or two and occasionally indulged in mild to moderate inebriation. He had long since realized that he was a slave to smoking.

There was even an occasional session of sex with one or another willing young lady. But this generally pleasant diversion was becoming noticeably less frequent. He had advanced from the sexual obsession of youth through the active pursuit of his twenties and the not so active thirties to his present situation, best described as interest considerably modified by a chronic suspicion that the matrimonial aspirations of a willing partner might be more important to him than the promise of a quick roll in the hay. In order for his citadel of bachelorhood to remain inviolate, he had to temper his biological urges with a good deal of caution. Or so he rationalized. On the other hand, maybe he was just getting old.

Hell, Brennan thought, he had no quarrel with marriage per se. His very livelihood was dependent upon a brisk birth rate. But, as good as marriage was to him, it was not for him.

Brennan had never consciously decided that he was going to forego marriage and family life. Rather, he had just never had time for it. His own jealous courtesan would not allow him the extravagance of participating in this most basic institution.

Oh, he was never lonely. He did have this mistress. And she was—still is—a demanding bitch. Medicine. And the price of her favors came very high indeed, at least as far as Dr. Patrick Brennan was concerned. She required endless hours of study. Practice, continuing adoration at her shrine, devoured the rest of his time and energies. His love of medicine had engulfed him, obsessed him, and made for a full, challenging, and usually satisfying way of life.

Lately, though, he had been wondering if he'd made the right choice. The fickle harlot that was medicine had shown him yet another side of the slavery that she demanded. There was heartbreak in her, and pathos, and the chronic despair of never really knowing her well. There was fatigue so deep and overwhelming that it at times seemed unbearable. And ingratitude. Further, what had at first seemed to be quite a satisfying degree of financial security succumbed to taxes at the end of each year, leaving only the good life, with no time or energy or means to enjoy it.

And finally, there were parents—the bane of every child specialist. The kids were good and beautiful, though often cruelly honest. Ah, but their immediate forebears—they were something else. There were all kinds of parents—good, bad, appreciative, unconcerned, dumb, smart, smart-assed, or downright bastardly. And there was even the vicious, baby-beating variety of parents. The logical extension of this line of thought led to the child-killing kind of parent that the yet unknown Mrs. Teal allegedly represented.

So lately he had begun to wonder, to speculate if it really was all worth it. This was a damn depressing thought for a man over forty. And even if it were all true, if he acknowledged the basic error of his life, just what in the hell could he do about it now? The substance of the whole problem was that he simply was no longer very happy.

So Patrick Brennan sat, apparently quiet and at peace. And inside he was a veritable cacophony of experience and expertise and emptiness.

Brennan's thoughts were interrupted by the abrupt realization that a man was standing in front of him. He was a middle-sized man in a gray suit and a white shirt. The man had both hands shoved in his hip pockets, so it was very easy to see the small holstered pistol attached to his belt.

Brennan leaped to his feet, smiled, and extended his hand. "Captain Miller? I'm Dr. Brennan."

The plainclothesman glanced at the doctor's hand, then shifted his eyes to Brennan's face. "Yeah. I'm Captain Miller."

Brennan withdrew his proffered hand and sat down again. He took Judge Waggoner's court order out of his briefcase and presented it to Miller.

Miller glanced at the document and muttered, "I heard a rumor about this, but I hoped it wasn't true."

"Why?"

"I'll tell you why. Because a beautiful little girl was tortured to death. What crime could be worse than that, Dr. Brennan? Can you in your wildest dreams imagine anything more cruel than that? Can you?"

"Well, Captain, I know —"

"Just a second, Dr. Brennan. There is one thing that is even more hideous than the death of that baby—the fact that the kid's own mother did the killing. God, it makes me sick to talk about it."

"Well, I'm sorry about that, Captain Miller," Brennan said quietly. "I'm sorry that this Teal case offends you. But if you'll

25

read that court order again, Miller, you'll find that it clearly states that I am to be given full cooperation in every aspect of the investigation of the Teal murder. You are the investigating officer. That paper says you will cooperate. The alternative is called contempt of court, so I suppose, even though it makes you sick, you're going to have to fill me in on the facts of the killing."

The policeman flung himself out of his chair and stomped over to a window. "Goddamn judge gets a guilty plea—guilty of murder. None of the usual deals. Guilty to the big one!" He whirled about, faster than Brennan thought he could have maneuvered, and slammed his fist down on the desk top. "But does that make the old son of a bitch happy? Hell no! He has to look this gift-horse in the mouth. He has to go get another headshrinker and see if he can't come up with some half-assed excuse for not sentencing poor misguided Mrs. Teal to life imprisonment. I'll never understand judges if I live to be a hundred."

Captain Miller flopped back into his chair and sighed loudly. Then in a more subdued voice, "No, Brennan, I'm just not overjoyed to see you here. Sorry about that."

"Captain Miller," Brennan began, "I hesitate to correct your brilliant deductive judgment, but I'm not a psychiatrist, or as you so cleverly phrased it, a headshrinker."

"What?" He paused. "What kind of a doctor are you then? Some other brand of psychomechanic?"

"I happen to be a pediatrician—a medical doctor that specializes in diseases of infants and children. I also happen to be an authority on the battered child syndrome—the complex problems of why a parent abuses a child, how the mistreatment affects the child, and what can be done about it. And that, Captain Miller, is why I am here.

"I realize that doesn't fit your preformed opinion of me or of my role in this case, and I realize that upsets you. Now I don't fit so easily into either of your two categories—black or white. I'm sorry for the mental inconvenience this no doubt causes you. However, Captain Miller, if I discover that your investigation consists of evidence manufactured to fit your simple-minded prejudgment of the Teal case, I will be not at all sorry to blow your whole investigation and all your damned prejudices to hell." Brennan paused, then added, "You see, Captain, we have a basic disagreement. I don't think this case is quite as simple as you'd like to make it."

The policeman was immobile. Finally he picked up his phone, dialed a single number, and said distinctly, "Bring me the file on the Teal killing."

There followed a period of apprehensive armistice while the policeman dispassionately briefed Brennan on the details of the Teal case.

The first indication to outsiders that all was not well in the Teal household had occurred on a weekday morning that past September. Jackie Teal, clothed only in her nightgown and robe, was seen wandering aimlessly around the neighborhood. She passed by the two homes immediately adjacent to her own, then meandered up onto the porch of the third house. Mrs. Teal just stood on the porch for several minutes, apparently doing nothing. Finally she rang the doorbell.

A Mrs. Lederle answered her chime to find herself confronted with a female automaton that merely stared at her when she asked the nature of this unexpected visit. Mrs. Lederle was not a friend of the Teals, so it took her a few moments to realize that this disheveled woman was her neighbor from down the block.

After what seemed like eons of elapsed time, Mrs. Teal blurted out that her baby had fallen and was injured. Would Mrs. Lederle please phone the fire department and ask them to send their ambulance to the Teal residence?

Mrs. Teal, suddenly infused with energy and purpose, then returned to her own home. Mrs. Lederle promptly made the call, and then began to wonder a bit. Why hadn't Mrs. Teal

27

used her own phone for the emergency message? Or at least the telephone of a closer neighbor? Then she thought of shock, and used that universal excuse for bizarre behavior to settle the question in her own mind. Thus any sinister interpretation of Mrs. Teal's activities was delayed until later, when her behavior pattern was reexamined in the light of subsequent developments.

The two-man crew of the Rossdale inhalator squad arrived at the Teal residence a few minutes later. Carrying their positive pressure oxygen system, the firemen hurried into the house through the unlocked front door. They were halfway through the neat little cottage before Jacqueline Teal knew of their presence. Curiously, they surprised her in the act of cleaning the bathroom floor. The squad leader later confided that his first thought on seeing the lady of the house down on her knees, busily scrubbing away, was that somebody had goofed and they'd come to the wrong address.

Jackie Teal was quick to allay this misconception. She said the baby was in her crib, and with a great deal of composure, she closed the bathroom door and led the rescue team to the door of the adjacent bedroom. The firemen pushed past her, making ready their oxygen equipment as they approached the red-haired infant lying perfectly still in her crib.

However, when they took a close look at her, all their activities abruptly ceased. Too late. This one was dead. Horribly dead.

The fireman and his assistant turned and slowly retraced their steps to the hallway. Mrs. Teal had neither moved nor spoken. The squad leader, Jeff Ostrowski, told Mrs. Teal very bluntly that her daughter was beyond any help they could give her. The woman said nothing. She did not cry. Ostrowski started to ask her what had happened to the little one, then thought better of it and followed his partner out to the ambulance.

While Ostrowski radioed headquarters to send the coroner

and the police to the Teal residence, his partner leaned heavily against the side of the truck and became violently sick.

After the briefing, Captain Miller took Brennan to see the coroner of Ross County, Dr. Karl Winston.

Dr. Winston's medical office was located in a small clinic just outside the downtown area.

A starched and efficient-looking nurse led Brennan and Miller through a crowded waiting room and rather reluctantly escorted them into the consultation room to await the arrival of Dr. Winston.

Several minutes later the obviously harried physician entered. He muttered on the evils of Mondays, greeted Captain Miller, and was in turn introduced to Brennan. "Very glad to meet you, Dr. Brennan. Of course I've heard of you. Read your articles on battered children. Matter of fact, I guess I'm partly responsible for your being here. The judge and I conspired a bit."

Winston failed to notice the fleeting expression of anger that passed over Miller's face, but Brennan caught it and knew its significance.

"Something about your waiting room tells me you are pressed, Doctor," Brennan said amicably. "Do you have time to fill me in on the Teal case now?"

"Sure. Let me get my file." The young physician—Brennan guessed him to be in his mid-thirties—took an envelope from his file cabinet. "I've got a cubbyhole office in the courthouse, but I find it much more convenient to keep the active files here. Now let's see. I was notified of the death of Helen Teal at 9:30 A.M. on Tuesday, September 12. I arrived at the scene about the same time the police got there—about 9:40. Grant and I took a quick look at the body. I checked her over briefly just to be sure she was dead.

"She was dead all right. Deader than hell. The corpse was covered up to the neck with a blanket, but was already getting cool. Let's see—rectal temperature ninety-four degrees at ten A.M. Partial rigor mortis already present. It usually comes on faster in kids. I estimated that her death, all factors considered, occurred at about seven or eight o'clock that morning.

"Little Helen's fatal injuries were obvious. Look over these pictures. You can see that her head really received a pounding. Note the traumatic exophthalmos of her right eye. Damn near punched it out. Bruises all over her face and scalp. These are obviously of varying ages, as were those on the rest of her body. Indicates previous trauma from repeated beatings. This view shows the fresh abrasions on her chin. Note the grossly deformed cranium due to the multiple fractures of her skull incurred during the final assault that morning.

"At autopsy the immediate cause of death was found to be acute bilateral subdural hematomas. She also sustained a degree of subarachnoid hemorrhage. There was further evidence of old, partially healed chronic subdurals.

"The skin bruises, old and new, were legion, near universal in their distribution over the surface of the body."

Dr. Winston handed Brennan a photograph of the corpse lying face down. On the child's back and shoulders were several recently inflicted, loop-shaped bruises.

"Did you find a lamp-cord whip?" Brennan asked.

"Yes," Miller answered grudgingly. "Found it in the garbage can out back. A little blood and traces of skin on the cord. Amateur attempt to hide the evidence."

"How about any skeletal evidence of abuse?"

"Plenty. And classic too."

Dr. Winston picked up another envelope, and fished out a number of black and gray negatives. He turned on his desktop view-box and the physicians reviewed the x-rays. These revealed multiple fractures of the skull, as well as fractures about the orbit of the right eye. The views of her skeletal survey disclosed an untreated break in her left humerus that, judging from the degree of callus present, must have been incurred about three to five weeks before her death. There was a fresh spiral fracture of the right radius, indicating a twisting injury to her forearm, as if the assailant had held the struggling child by the arm while administering a whipping.

The radiographs also showed many other minor skeletal injuries, all in different stages of healing. Even at the time of her death, Helen Teal's body was attempting to repair the damage from previous beatings.

Neither Brennan nor Miller attempted to make conversation as they drove away from their session with the coroner. The doctor was completely preoccupied with his consideration of all the new information he had obtained.

Brennan thought about Mrs. Teal and other parents like her. Too bad they couldn't all be at least adequate parents. It was, in fact, too bad that anyone, regardless of his parental abilities, could, by the simple accident of procreation, become loosely endowed with the title of mother or father.

This excruciating parody of parenthood was certainly nothing new to Dr. Brennan. He enjoyed the sometimes dubious honor of having established himself in pediatric circles as an authority on the very subject, so tragically exemplified by the death of two-year-old Helen Teal. Why? There were other facets of his specialty that were pleasant and rewarding. Like well-baby care. Beautiful. Even the routine acute illnesses of children, so quick in onset, were usually just as sudden in their cure. These and many other aspects of pediatric medicine were just fine. But not child abuse.

On the surface, it seemed hopeless. Yet Brennan knew that the often desperate plight of the involved babies and children required urgent attention. They got this help, or too often they ended up prematurely dead. Like little Helen. And they all had a right to live. So then it didn't make much difference if Dr. Patrick Brennan, or any other physician for that matter, found child abuse depressing.

31

The need for help was there. It existed. It was a part of reality. And Brennan had realized long ago that he had to do something about the whole damn mess. Consequently, he found himself caught up in the study of the morbid pathology of what had been christened the Battered Child Syndrome.

It was a desperately urgent and demanding field of study. A vast amount of research and endless study were necessary prerequisites to understanding the problem. But with this knowledge, effective help for the children and parents just might evolve. And then the little ones need suffer no more.

"What was Mrs. Teal's reaction to your discovery of her murdered child?" Brennan asked Miller after they were once again seated in the policeman's office.

"Initially she tried to say that the child had fallen down the basement stairs. When we blew that line she said that a strange man had entered the house early that morning, beaten poor Helen, and then threatened to return and do the same to the four-year-old girl, as well as to Mrs. Teal herself if she didn't keep quiet."

The doctor lit a cigarette, then continued the questioning. "How did you get the truth out of her?"

"It was easy. The four-year-old girl was there in the house that morning. She had been playing quietly in the kitchen throughout all the confusion and mess. I simply asked her who had hurt Helen. She told me that her mother had whipped Helen when she peed in her pants. The mother heard the kid tell me and started screeching and blubbering and groaning and carrying on. After a while, she quieted down and gave us a very nice confession. She confessed verbally at home. Later she signed this typed statement here at the station. Here's a copy."

"Is this an admissible confession?" Brennan asked.

"Yes, Doctor. We told the bitch all about her ever-lovin'

rights regarding any and all possible incrimination of her precious self, and legal representation, and all that crap."

Brennan could barely contain his dislike of Miller. He crushed out his cigarette and directed his attention to the confession. It was a carbon copy of a typed statement that had obviously been prepared in a hurry—before Mrs. Teal could change her mind. Consequently all corrections were initialed J.T. At the end it was signed "Jacqueline Teal" and witnessed by Grant Miller and a lady named Holt—probably the stenographer.

On closer examination Brennan noticed that there were actually two statements. The second was titled "Further Questioning and Responses of Jacqueline Teal." It too was signed and witnessed. Holding one in either hand, the physician looked quizzically at Captain Miller.

"The first is her confession of the actual killing. We wanted to get that typed up and properly signed before she had a chance to become uncooperative. The second concerns her past mistreatment of Helen. In the end she was truly very obliging—she signed both of them."

The actual confession of the murder was much as Brennan had expected it to be from his previous experience with child abusers. Mrs. Teal said her daughter Helen had gotten up before seven A.M. on that September morning. While preparing breakfast for the two girls, Mrs. Teal noted that Helen suddenly hesitated in her busy wanderings about the kitchen and deliberately wet her panties. Right there in the middle of her clean kitchen. This naturally infuriated Jackie. She grabbed the first handy weapon—it happened to be the cord of the coffee pot—and proceeded to whip the living hell out of Helen. She was sure that her urination was yet another example of Helen's chronic defiance of her mother.

After thrashing Helen soundly, Mrs. Teal dragged the screaming child into the bathroom and slammed her down on the potty chair. The enraged mother intended to make the brat sit there until she realized that no more bladder or bowel "accidents" were going to be tolerated in the Teal household.

Unfortunately the hurt and terrified two-year-old could think only of escape. She tried to run. This proved to be a fatal error. Jackie Teal interpreted her daughter's attempt to flee as an act of open defiance. The little girl found herself hurled back on the potty. Again her reflexes demanded escape. Almost immediately she was up and off again. Again she was thrown backwards. But this time the potty chair toppled over and Helen crashed into the wall.

The next thing Mrs. Teal could remember, according to her confession, was that she was straddling Helen's body battering her head against the bathroom floor.

Mrs. Teal then saw that something was wrong with her daughter's right eye. And her breathing seemed funny—sort of snorey. There was a little blood. But, thank God, the kid had quit her damn screaming.

She then put the baby back into her crib and pulled a cover over her.

Jacqueline, now that her wrath was satiated, returned to her kitchen and finished cooking breakfast for herself and her oldest child.

Later, she did not know just when, she returned to the bedroom to check on Helen. All was quiet. No more snoring. Then Mrs. Teal realized that there were no breathing sounds at all. Her daughter looked very queer. She'd better get some help. Jackie was apparently frightened now, for her girl and for herself. She became confused in her immediate purpose. She should get something or do something. But what? How?

The next thing Mrs. Teal could recall, she was outside her own house, standing on a neighbor's porch in her night clothes. She asked this person, she couldn't remember just who it was—just a neighbor—at any rate, she asked her to call for help. For Helen.

Back home, she decided to clean up the mess in the bathroom before any strangers came. Jackie believed in keeping a neat house.

Yes, she knew that she had done wrong. She realized that she had killed little Helen. But she didn't mean to do that. Didn't mean to kill her. Or even to hurt her. She was only attempting to do what was right. That child was always taunting her. Helen knew better than to wet herself. But she did that sort of thing on purpose—just to provoke her mother.

Wasn't it a mother's job to train her children? Teach them right from wrong? That's all Jackie Teal was trying to do. And Helen needed discipline. She had a wild streak in her. She had to learn obedience, didn't she? And it was a mother's duty to correct her.

It was, therefore, all an accident. Jackie had not wanted to kill her child. She had wanted to help her. It was all a horrible accident.

That was the substance of the "confession."

Brennan then turned his attention to the addendum, or the further responses of Mrs. Teal to the questions of Captain Miller. This document proved to be an even more repulsive postscript to the murder. It also reflected the fact that once Miller had the signed testimony of guilt in hand, he felt he could afford the luxury of trying to clarify the pertinent events that preceded the killing.

Miller's intention was obvious. He was trying to prove that the old injuries, revealed by the forensic examination of the corpse, were in fact physical evidence of premeditation of homicidal assault, especially when considered in light of the subsequent fact of the death itself.

For instance, the obviously untreated fracture of her arm— how did that happen? Mrs. Teal answered, of course, that she knew nothing about it. But if Miller said it was broken, then it must have been broken. The child probably fell. Busted it then. She fell a lot.

Same answer about the multiple external bruises of varying

ages. She was an unsteady little girl. She fell out of bed, fell while playing, and was prone to physical altercations with her older sister.

How about medical care for these injuries? Was there ever an attempt made to see a doctor? Well, no. But the girl didn't complain. She didn't seem to be injured seriously enough to require professional treatment. How was the mother to know this was indicated? Did they expect her to be an expert in the diagnosis of all the "accidental" injuries of children? Kids fall all the time.

At this point it occurred to Dr. Brennan that in his private practice mothers damn near overwhelmed him with their requests for advice concerning their children's injuries, most of which were decidedly trivial in comparison with the insults that Helen Teal had sustained. Brennan was a devout believer in mothers' intuition, a powerful and effective force working for the safety and well-being of their offspring. Jacqueline Teal's confession, however, seemed to deny the very existence of this mothering instinct. Yet her denial of responsibility as a mother was the manifestation of another type of very powerful instinctive behavior—that of self-preservation.

Brennan could see that Jackie Teal was revealing a great deal more about herself than she realized or wanted to. He recognized that the mother demanded behavior that was much too advanced for her two-year-old daughter. She decreed premature potty training, proscribed crying, and demanded compliance and servitude. Yet the mother demonstrated by word and deed that she thought it quite all right to behave like a vindictive child herself. She could drop all restraint. She could attack. And she could kill.

It made Brennan wonder just who was expected to be the mother and who the infant in the perverted dramatis personae of this farce-turned-tragedy.

"May I keep these copies, Captain?"

36

"Sure, Doc. Is there any other little thing I can do? To help you?"

"Your sarcasm again shows your marked tendency toward prejudgment, Officer."

Miller slammed the Teal case file onto his desk. Leaning across the desk top in a downright menacing manner, he shouted, "Jesus Christ! You made out of stone or something? How the hell can you sit there so damn smug after what you've seen and read this afternoon?" Shaking his head, he collapsed back into his chair.

"Captain Miller, I was not called to Rossdale to join a lynch mob. And if you think that merely because I'm trying to understand this case means that I'm not sick to my stomach and mad as hell about what's happened, then you've made still another error in judgment.

"Now, Captain, I have to ask you a few more questions— then I'll leave you to your vindictive fuming.

"What about Mr. Teal? Where was he while all this was going on?"

"Mr. and Mrs. Teal were separated," Miller replied in a resigned monotone. "James Teal moved out a few weeks before the murder. He moved back to Chicago, where this whole misbegotten family lived before they came here. He left his wife because she was mistreating the kids—particularly their second child, Helen."

"Interesting." Dr. Brennan retrieved his case and coat. "Mr. Teal recognized the child abuse and it scared him. So he ran away. Should be able to infer a little something about what kind of a husband and father he was."

"Yeah, looks like they made a really lovely couple. Like a black widow spider and her savory mate. Only he escaped his fate, so she took it out on Helen."

CHAPTER IV

Patrick Brennan lay fully clothed on the bed in his motel room. The lights were off. His eyes were closed, but he was not asleep. He was trying to recover from a severe tension headache.

The phone rang. "Brennan here."

"Dr. Brennan?"

"Yes."

"You don't know me, Doctor. My name is Lawrence Mc-Neill. I've come to Rossdale to see you."

"Why, Mr. McNeill?"

"It's rather a long story, Dr. Brennan. I'm afraid we can't do it justice over the phone. I'm a vice-president of Pembroke Drugs. I'm sure that suggests the nature of my mission."

"Damn. Not that today, too," Brennan mumbled.

"What was that, sir?"

"Nothing. Just what is it you want of me, Mr. McNeill? I'm sure Pembroke Drugs knows my position in the whole miserable controversy. What would be gained by our hashing it out all over again?"

"It is very difficult to settle these matters by letter, or even through third parties such as the Food and Drug people. All I ask is the opportunity to review the matter with you. That way we can both work toward a reasonable solution. Doctor, I know a physician with your fine reputation in pediatric circles has to be a reasonable man. You'll find me quite a reasonable fellow, too. And I have come a very long way specifically to see you. May I suggest you join me for dinner and a frank discussion this evening? We can meet here in the motel dining room if you like."

"Okay, Mr. McNeill. What time?"

"Shall we say seven?"

"Sounds reasonable."

"Sir?"

"That's just fine, Mr. McNeill. Meet you in the bar at seven. Good-bye." He cradled the telephone, lay down again, and tried to think of absolutely nothing.

Patrick Brennan's headache had evaporated by the time he inquired for a Mr. McNeill in the bar. Almost immediately a tall, well-dressed man approached him. "I'm Lawrence Mc-Neill," he said with smiling assurance. McNeill was suntanned and lean except for a slight paunch which was successfully camouflaged by expert tailoring. He smoothly escorted Brennan to a table and ordered two Manhattans.

At home, Brennan rarely had a Manhattan or martini before his dinner. He preferred a milder aperitif to heighten his appreciation of Mrs. Collins's culinary talents. Mrs. Collins was an elderly Negress who came limping into his apartment three afternoons a week, did a little light, predictably ineffectual cleaning, and prepared his dinner. Her Pintadeaux aux Cerises was superb, especially when enhanced with a cold bottle of Bennkastler Doktor Spatlese from his wine closet. And when Mrs. Collins prepared her Boeuf Bourguignonne, the physician's praises of her artistry knew no limits.

Brennan harbored no illusions about small-town motel dining. So he drank his Manhattan, confirmed the fact that the only French word on the menu was filet, and ordered the steak. At least Midwestern corn-fed beef was still the best in the world.

Later, as the meal progressed, McNeill began to edge the conversation into matters of more substance.

"Dr. Brennan, I feel it would be best if you would give me a brief summary of your position on our product Gastropep. Then we'll both know exactly what we're talking about, and neither of us will make any erroneous assumptions that might amplify our differences."

Brennan laid down his knife and fork, leaned forward, and said, "My position is quite simple, Mr. McNeill. Gastropep is not a safe product for children. You people are continually hawking the damn stuff as a sure-fire cure for an upset stomach. You aim this propaganda at parents for the treatment of any and all stomach disorders their offspring might have. Then for the necessary insurance, you say—in very small print—'if symptoms are not relieved in a reasonable time, consult your physician.' Now that is all very fine. Except that your product is simply not safe. It has killed children and, unless you change your formula, will do so again."

"All right, Dr. Brennan," McNeill replied with a condescending smile. "Now please consider our position. We have marketed this product for generations. Literally millions of people have used Gastropep. And they found it to be not only harmless but also an excellent remedy for mild stomach upset and diarrhea. The formula is old and of unquestionable safety."

"Well, that pretty well delineates the battle lines."

"Then tell me, Doctor, why you disagree."

"You've surely read my correspondence on this, Mr. McNeill. You must be acquainted with the facts of my objections."

"Of course, Doctor. I've read it all. And the very fact that I have come all this way to seek you out shows how seriously we at Pembroke Drugs consider your allegations. But, again, I feel a full and frank discussion between the two of us is essential, even though it may be a bit repetitious."

"Very well, Mr. McNeill. I will recite for you the sad tale that has led to our meeting tonight." Brennan lit a cigarette,

41

then added, "But it's a saga of epic proportions, so bear with me."

"Please go ahead, Doctor." McNeill signaled the waitress for coffee.

Brennan waited for the coffee to arrive, then began to speak. "It all began many years ago. A very nice couple in a suburb of St. Louis had a baby. A little girl. They christened her Robin. Robin Warren. They selected me as the pediatrician for their only daughter—only child, for that matter."

"They showed good judgment." McNeill's smile was warm, fetching, and only slightly phony.

"Thank you. At any rate, Mr. McNeill, the Warrens were very happy with each other and with their daughter. They were not wealthy people, but they provided all they thought was necessary and desirable for their little girl. This included good pediatric supervision. Consequently, over the years, I got to know Robin and her family rather well.

"The Warrens were sensible parents. Not easy to panic, not overprotective. Every time Robin would get some little illness, they exercised what I believe was quite good judgment in her management. If they could handle it with symptomatic care, they did. If they needed me, they called. All this worked out very well until last year."

Brennan paused as if he were reluctant to go on. He ground his cigarette into the ashtray and methodically extinguished every smouldering particle of ash. He picked up his cup of coffee, leaned back in his chair and continued. "One day last spring Robin Warren got sick. Nothing alarming. Just seemed to be one of those so-called stomach viruses or intestinal flu things. That name covers a lot of sins, but I'm afraid it's here to stay.

"Nevertheless, Mrs. Warren put her daughter to bed. Robin had abdominal cramps, some nausea, and one or two episodes of vomiting. This subsided, but was followed by mild diarrhea. No different from what she and all six-year-olds have experienced many times in the past. Mrs. Warren knew that the best treatment for this illness was dietary. She gave Robin clear sweet liquids, followed by skim milk, and then a low-fat diet several hours after the nausea and vomiting subsided. Everything was going along fine. Just fine.

"Unfortunately, Mr. Warren happened to telephone before he came home. The parents discussed the girl's illness. In the course of their conversation they realized their unpardonable sin. Robin had not received any medicine as yet.

"Now, I don't have to tell you how overly impressed the American public is with the idea that if you are sick, you've got to take some medicine. It's part of the magic. Every time you pick up a paper, or a magazine, or turn on your radio or T.V., you're bombarded with 'medicinitis'. You have to take something for everything from tired blood to a sluggish liver, whatever the hell that is. Our society is definitely drug oriented. And so were the poor Warrens.

"Consequently, Mr. Warren stopped at a supermarket on his way home that evening and purchased a bottle of refreshing, relieving, good tasting Gastropep. The Warrens read the instructions very carefully. They shook the bottle thoroughly, just as directed. Then they gave the damn stuff to their daughter. Precisely as directed.

"After several hours — You sure you want to hear all of this, Mr. McNeill?"

"Yes, Doctor. Please continue."

"Okay. Now, let's see. Later that night Robin complained of more abdominal cramps. As you recall, this symptom had disappeared earlier. At about one in the morning Robin vomited again. The parents were still not alarmed, mind you. They decided she just needed a little more treatment—a little more medicine. So they gave her another dose of Gastropep.

"By five in the morning they could see that their little girl was really very ill. She was moaning intermittently and be-

43

coming very disturbed—thrashing about, completely disoriented. That's when they called me.

"When I examined Robin in the emergency room of the hospital—this was about 5:45 that morning—I found my little friend to be desperately ill. She was quite wild, babbling incoherently, in excruciating pain. She would hold her head, grab her belly, then pathetically probe somewhere else in a vain search for relief. The physical examination failed to provide any adequate diagnosis compatible with her obviously catastrophic symptoms. The only specifically abnormal physical finding was widely dilated pupils.

"Now, Mr. McNeill, this is rather common in an overdosage, or idiosyncrasy, to atropine-like drugs. And, as I'm sure you know, such compounds are frequently found in stomach medications. So I quizzed the parents at great length about what medicine they had given Robin. Both adamantly denied giving her anything other than Gastropep.

"A quick check of a clinical toxicology book in the hospital's Poison Control Center revealed that Gastropep contained no atropine derivatives of any kind. So I thought that it was off the hook as far as any etiological relationship to Robin's illness was concerned."

"Thank God," McNeill said.

"Hold it. Your relief is premature." Brennan looked suspiciously at his companion. "Are you sure you read the data I sent to Pembroke on all this?"

"Of course. Then —?"

"The case made no sense. No sense at all. Her symptoms were so suggestive of some kind of acute poisoning that for a while there I actually doubted the honesty of Robin's parents. I thought they might have given her some secret home remedy that they felt guilty about. At any rate, I sent Mrs. Warren home to check all the drugs that she kept in the house, just to be sure that Robin hadn't taken something toxic on her own. She was a little old for that sort of behavior, but I had to explore all the possibilities. As an afterthought I asked her to bring that bottle of Gastropep to me. I was not at all suspicious of your product. I don't really know why I asked her to bring it.

"For a while I was busy getting Robin started on appropriate symptomatic treatment and making further efforts at diagnosis. I ordered an analysis of her cerebro-spinal fluid for evidence of meningitis or encephalitis—inflammation of the brain. These studies were negative.

"The therapy was largely to relieve her pain and to provide general supportive measures. I got an intravenous going to maintain her hydration. But I just couldn't get the idea of acute poisoning out of my mind. So I ordered an indwelling catheter to be inserted into her urinary bladder. We collected and saved all her urine—froze it—for later lab tests for any toxins it might contain. We did the same with her stomach contents, obtained by putting a plastic tube through her nose and throat, passing it into her stomach, and suctioning out the gastric contents. Also took samples of her blood for virus studies, just in case this illness represented some weird viremia. I ordered regular bacterial cultures of her blood. I also saved a blood specimen for toxicology. I hate to sound so clinical, but in light of subsequent developments, all this proved to be invaluable."

"You were very thorough," McNeill commented, but his voice betrayed a lack of enthusiasm for the physician's diagnostic efforts in this particular case.

Brennan sensed this and ignored it. He continued. "This took a couple of hours of damn hard work on my part and the devoted efforts of several pediatric nurses. All the while Robin was getting sicker. Her pain wasn't lessened by the safe doses of narcotics. Her spasms became more violent and more frequent. And I could do nothing to help. Nothing.

"Robin could no longer talk. But she could communicate with me with her eyes, Mr. McNeill. Her big, brown, overly dilated eyes. She told me very eloquently how great her pain was. She begged me to help her, to make the pain go away.

"McNeill, I could read all this and more in that tortured child's eyes. Read it too loud and too clear. I could recognize that she was saying that magic word of childhood—please— in her prayer to me. And, for all the relief I was giving her, I might just as well have stayed in bed that miserable morning."

Dramatic son of a bitch, McNeill thought.

Brennan finished his now tepid coffee and with an obvious effort managed to shift into a more subdued tone. "I was still trying to fathom this bizarre illness when Robin's mother returned. The search for unknown poisons at home was fruitless. But I had the shiny bottle of Gastropep in my hand.

"For want of any other brilliant mental machinations, I found myself reading the small print on the label of your stomach medicine. I noted one ingredient in Gastropep that I was unfamiliar with. I had heard of the drug, but couldn't recall much about it. So I headed for the poison files again— and I hit pay dirt right off. I had it! I had found the information that explained Robin's complete clinical picture.

"The drug I am referring to is called salol. Its chemical name is phenyl salicylate.

"Now, let me just dwell for a minute on this salol, or phenyl salicylate. When ingested, it may undergo a chemical reaction called hydrolysis and break down into two ingredients within the body. One is a kind of salicylate, of which aspirin is the most familiar form. The other derivative is phenol. Now, Mr. McNeill, phenol is more commonly called carbolic acid—one of the most powerful poisons known to man. It is a protoplasmic poison—toxic to all the cells of the body. All the cells —brain, heart, lung, liver, muscle, blood, bone, skin—everything. And it kills these cells, Mr. McNeill. Some of them we can spare. But some of these cells that are killed we can't spare. And when these individual vital cells die, the organism dies.

46

"And that, Mr. McNeill, is just what my little friend Robin proceeded to do."

McNeill looked as if he were about to say something, but Brennan interrupted. "I think I need a drink. Something stronger than this cold coffee, Mr. McNeill. Shall we repair to the bar to finish this loathsome tale?"

They obtained after-dinner drinks and Brennan continued. "Back to my patient. I got ahead of the story there. I now had a working diagnosis for Robin's illness. She was in the excitement phase of phenol poisoning. I knew then what to expect. And I got it.

"Her agitation and delirium soon progressed to severe convulsions. Uncontrollable generalized seizures. One right on top of the last one. Then there came the anticipated and blessed coma. This was followed by respiratory paralysis. I kept her going on a respirator and other supportive measures for a while longer. She was what we call a heart-lung preparation. A vegetable. The shell of a once beautiful child, with a dying or dead brain. A zombie, kept alive—if you can call it life—by mechanical resuscitative devices.

"Finally, her heart yielded to this relentless poison. She died very early the following morning.

"Death is usually considered to be the nemesis of the medical man, Mr. McNeill, but not always. Sometimes death can be a friend. As it was that morning. I had seen the pain, the literal living hell that Robin went through, and I knew that she had suffered irreversible damage. So her death was a blessing—a kindness to both of us." Brennan stared blankly for a second, then finished his drink.

McNeill's expression was appropriately softened, conveying sympathy, understanding. "I can see that it was an extremely trying experience for you, Doctor. I can also see that you really believe that our product was responsible for this tragedy, but —"

"Do you doubt it, McNeill?" Brennan interrupted sharply.

He was surprised by his own uncharacteristic display of anger. He sighed, then continued more calmly. "I suppose you do. That's your job. But I'm not interested in getting Pembroke Drugs to admit any liability. I'm not that naive. I've had only two limited goals in respect to your product since the outset."

"And these are?"

"First, to acquaint my colleagues with the danger of serious complications when Gastropep is used. Second, to get Pembroke Drugs to take that goddamn salol out of their formula. That's all."

"That's all, you say. That's all! Well, Doctor, believe me, that's a hell of a lot!" McNeill was furious and made no attempt to appear otherwise.

"You have one damn isolated case. You believe that our product caused this death. One case out of literally generations of youngsters who have taken our medicine and experienced only relief of their symptoms."

Seeing that his outburst had had no effect on the physician, McNeill made an abrupt change in his approach. He leaned across the table and continued in a tone of voice that implied intimacy and understanding. "Now Doctor, you have to be reasonable. Surely you've had bad reactions to medications in the past—penicillin allergy, many others. You wouldn't expect those drug manufacturers to withdraw or change their products because of these occasional poor responses or side effects, would you?"

"No, I would not, Mr. McNeill. And it's true that any physician will experience his share of allergic, anaphylactic, and idiosyncratic reactions. Few if any drugs escape the occasional backlash effect. But there is a subtle difference involved here. Those other drugs are generally valuable tools that the physician uses to combat illness and death. Can you say the same about salol?"

"Why, our product has enjoyed success for many, many years. I could show you sales figures that would astound you."

"Hold it. You cannot equate safety and usefulness with sales figures, McNeill. I know that your product contains salol for the simple reason that it has been successful for so long. When Gastropep was originally formulated, salol was a preparation commonly used for upset stomachs. And in that same era, leeches were used to treat just about everything. You, sir, would flee in fear and haste from any physician who threatened to slap a leech on you today. True?"

"Well, yes. Of course. But —"

"One moment please. I have done a tremendous amount of research on this subject. I found all sorts of authorities who will tell you that salol has absolutely no value in the medical treatment of anything. No value at all. It is simply a dangerous holdover from that period of our history when the materia medica of the doctor was probably a greater threat to the well-being of his patient than was the illness or disease to be treated.

"Think how many people died of strychnine poisoning because it was prescribed as a remedy for just about anything from syphilis to a runny nose. Now it has largely disappeared, even from the list of proprietary drugs. Well, your salol is in the same category as strychnine. It does no good. It is still in the Gastropep formula because it always has been. And it is retained only because the brainwashed public continues to buy your very successfully promoted product. Even though it kills kids."

McNeill, now on the defensive, sensed a flaw in the doctor's argument. "Assuming you are right, Dr. Brennan. And this is only an assumption, mind you, for the sake of our discussion. You say it kills kids. You use the plural. Yet you have only one case. A single case where you say Gastropep was a lethal agent. Would this not suggest an unusual reaction on the part of that little girl, rather than an unsafe drug per se?"

"Mr. McNeill, I didn't assume anything. I know that your brand of carbolic acid killed Robin Warren. I could sense

49

poisoning from the first moment I saw her—long before I had an established working diagnosis. So I saved all the urine, blood, vomitus, et cetera. After her death, additional specimens were obtained and more information was revealed by the autopsy.

"All this was submitted to expert toxicological analysis. We proved the presence of salol in her intestines, and phenol in her organs and urine. We further analyzed the bottle of Gastropep and were able to show that it had just what you people call the right amount of salol in it. So there is no assumption involved here."

McNeill started to speak but Brennan raised his hand and continued, "Now, just a second more, please. Then I'll shut up and listen. You hopefully say 'one case.' But it isn't just one case—not anymore!

"As you know, I couldn't get very much reaction out of your company when I first contacted you people about Robin's death. Then I wrote an article on illness that was published in a pediatric journal, and you all got very nervous. The FDA got nervous too."

"That's just it, Dr. Brennan," McNeill interrupted. "The Food and Drug people did investigate the Warren girl's case. And they took no action. They dropped it."

"True," Brennan admitted. "But why?"

"What do you mean, why?" The vice-president's tone did little to conceal his exasperation at the professorial attitude he now detected in Brennan. "Because they obviously felt your allegation had no merit. Why else?"

"Did they tell you that, McNeill? Did they send you any kind of a report to that effect? Let me see it. I'd like to read it."

"Of course not." McNeill involuntarily recoiled from the physician.

"Well, how the hell do you know so much about their conclusions?" Brennan countered.

"We've had some informal contact with the Food and Drug

people. About your allegations. Unofficially, of course."

"Unofficially, my ass," Brennan sneered. "Why unofficially? Why informal? They sent a man around to see me. 'Investigator', he was labeled. They're big on labeling, you know. He made a show of going through my file, checking with the county medical examiner. He left promising great things to come. Called back a few times for clarification of this or that aspect of the case. Then nothing."

"The 'nothing' should tell you something, Dr. Brennan."

"Matter of fact, it does, McNeill. Rather, I should say, it smells of something."

Oh Christ, McNeill thought. I've stepped in it now.

"No curiosity, Mr. McNeill? Never mind. I'll explain anyway." Brennan lowered his voice to the proper conspiratorial level. "The nothing to which you referred, Mr. McNeill, suggests a payoff."

"If you're suggesting for one moment," McNeill sputtered angrily, "that Pembroke Drugs would bribe —"

"Did you?"

"What?"

"Bribe anybody?"

"Goddamn it, Brennan," the executive expostulated. He paused long enough to regain his self control. "What kind of animals do you think we are?"

"Kid killers."

"Oh, Jesus Christ," McNeill mumbled with ill-concealed disgust.

"What the hell am I supposed to believe? The FDA was all ready to take action. Then, without a by-your-leave, they suddenly drop the whole matter. They don't drop any ax they have to grind with the ethical pharmaceutical houses—and rightly so if they're correct in their criticism.

"I've been around long enough to remember, for example, when they piously pointed out that injectable iron caused malignant tumors in rats. Knocked a very valuable drug off

51

the market for several years, despite the fact that it was repeatedly stressed to them that their dosage in rats was astronomical in relation to what we used in humans.

"How many kids died in those withdrawn years, McNeill? We've known for a long time that some parents don't care enough about their kids to give them medicine even when it's badly needed. In a severe iron deficiency anemia case, the injectable iron was often life saving. How many succumbed to parental indifference when this very valuable drug was taken from us?

"They kick the hell out of the food people, too. But you guys, you non-prescription manufacturers with the do-nothing products, you people who spend millions for advertising and nothing for research or safety, you are the untouchables.

"I wonder why this is, Mr. McNeill, and I suspect others are beginning to wonder, too. Specifically, Senator Black's committee is scheduling hearings on the whole subject of over-the-counter drugs—their safety, efficacy, and cost. I'm scheduled to chat with them about Gastropep.

"But, more to the point, my pediatric colleagues read that article I published. And it made them start wondering about some similar patients they had seen. And it made them alert to the possibility that Gastropep might not be the innocuous preparation we had all assumed it to be for so long. Hell, the average pediatrician felt that this was the type of medication whose only value lay in the fact that it kept the parent busy and answered his need to do something, to give a medicine, while the proper diet and mother nature proceeded to get the patient well.

"But no longer do they smile so tolerantly on your Gastropep, Mr. McNeill. Now they suspect it! And when the isolated case presents itself, they investigate it. And in a fair number of these, the doctors are indicting your compound as a killer."

Brennan leaned toward his nervous companion and quietly

confided, "I personally know of five well-documented cases, soon to be reported in the pediatric literature, that confirm my findings completely. And this is all just a beginning, Mr. McNeill. I think it is safe to say that Pembroke Drugs is going to have quite a few problems with Gastropep in the future."

McNeill was now a very disturbed man. "Jesus Christ, do you have any idea what it would cost us to change that formula? Why, we would have to call back every bottle, throw it away, and replace it. To say nothing of regearing our whole production setup. Do you realize that would mean instant bankruptcy?"

"I don't particularly give a damn, McNeill. Now let me ask you a question. Do you have any idea how many children are rotting away in graveyards because of your product? And because gullible parents and their doctors and you people are too stupid to recognize the danger of your product?"

Lawrence McNeill was finding it difficult to suppress his anger. This physician was totally unreasonable. Pembroke Drugs had a gold mine in Gastropep, and he shared in it. It cost only a few cents a bottle to make the stuff and a few more cents for advertising and promotion. A fat net profit resulted from every bottle that was sold. Too damn bad if there was an occasional unfortunate reaction.

McNeill prided himself on being a fast thinker, one who could get to the very heart of a problem and come up with a solution. Now, as he ordered another round of drinks, he was outwardly more composed, but his mind was searching like a computer for the key that would remove this threat to the company. There had to be a way out of all this. This guy had to be stopped—fast.

McNeill could cheerfully cut the balls off the nosey columnist who had picked up Brennan's paper in that damn pediatric journal. Christ, these few puffed-up professionals could go around knocking Gastropep all their productive lives, and it wouldn't make a dent in the sales figures.

53

People looked to the buck, the cheap way out. This the medics didn't understand. It was simple psychology—too simple for the over-educated medical profession to imagine. People would gladly pay a couple of bills for a bottle of Gastropep. Hell of a lot cheaper, the average slob reasoned, than keeping his doctor in a Cadillac.

But the article in the Seattle newspaper, that was something else. And Pembroke's clipping service had found it for him. McNeill prayed the news bureaus wouldn't pick it up. It had appeared a couple of weeks ago. So far so good.

Just let any of the big guys put it out on the wire, and Gastropep was finished. Even if the slobs didn't read the papers, the networks would demolish Pembroke without batting an eye—despite the fact that the company spent millions on T.V. promotion every year.

That's what had put Lawrence McNeill on an airplane, trailing this dumb pediatrician all the way to godforsaken Rossdale. Brennan sure as hell wasn't that important. He was just one more itch to be scratched at leisure. Even his glorious pediatric article was a bunch of bullshit. Who the hell would read it? Who even knew of its existence?

But the news media—even that silly West-coast health writer who'd ferreted it out of the pediatric literature—that was something to worry about. That scared the hell out of the whole executive hierarchy at Pembroke Drugs. If any reporter got to Brennan personally, they'd be finished. That combination would flush Gastropep, and Lawrence McNeill, right down the toilet.

So he could not afford to think of losing here. Look what had happened to that soup company when the Food and Drug people yelled botulism. Right down the drain.

The FDA was getting a little touchy about over-the-counter drugs anyway. Promised investigations in low-key press releases, that sort of thing. But he wasn't really concerned about them. He'd heard their promises before. Anyway, it was an election year. And what screw-ball would want to jeopardize the political contributions of a whole industry by instigating investigations at such a sensitive time. No, Mc-Neill could cope with the FDA, but Senator Black's committee—that was something else. He had to turn off this bastard Brennan.

The drinks arrived. The blessed respite was over. He would keep Brennan talking. Something would come up. It had to.

"Doctor, I appreciate you taking your valuable time to brief me personally. And I appreciate your being so candid with me. I think I have a much better understanding of the total situation now. Of course I still have some problems, but I feel—"

"We all still have plenty of problems, Mr. McNeill," Brennan muttered unenthusiastically. He was obviously exhausted and eager to end the conversation.

"I'll just bet. You up here working, Doctor? Or just trying to get away from the telephone for a few days?"

"Both."

"Not working on the Gastropep thing are you?" McNeill's voice betrayed his tension.

"No. Not at all. I'm here on a consultative thing. Just for a few days. Then back to the grind."

"Must be rough being a pediatrician. Busy all day. Lots of night calls, too, I imagine. And it's not one of the better paying medical specialties, is it?"

"Pediatrics has the dubious honor of being at the very bottom of the list when you rate the medical specialties according to the average financial return."

"Ever think of giving it up? Trying something else?" There it was. The key question was loosely, casually thrown out.

"Sure. I guess everyone does. At least every pediatrician does when he becomes sufficiently exhausted." Brennan could not suppress a yawn. "Speaking of exhaustion, I'm beat, Mr.

McNeill. This has been one hell of a long day. Here, let me get the check for these drinks."

"Nonsense, you're my guest tonight." He paid the bar tab in spite of the physician's protests. "I'm tired, too, but thanks again for your time and conversation. You going to be here in Rossdale very long?"

They were now walking toward their respective rooms. Patrick Brennan was extremely sleepy and slightly inebriated. "What? No. Just till Friday.

"Here's where I leave you, Mr. McNeill. Thanks again for the drinks and the dinner. Good night."

"Don't mention it. It's been an experience for me. Educational. Good night, Doctor." They parted and McNeill walked on toward his motel room.

He whistled a nameless tune. He was feeling much more confident now that he had an idea. Already he was starting to work out all the details. Of course he would need the approval of his boss, Silas Camp. But it could work if it were sprung on the doctor in just the right way. If this failed, they would have to come up with an alternative—a more drastic alternative, perhaps, but one that would work. He would see to that.

There was one hell of a lot riding on this particular victory, as far as he and his were concerned. His son, Barney, a graduate student at the Harvard Business School, would be assured of continuing his education. His wife, bless her frigid soul, could keep up the rich-bitch front that seemed to sustain her.

As for himself, well, there was a lot he'd hate to risk. Like Sarah, his current little friend, who was waiting patiently for him in their motel room. He knew her pretty well—well enough to know that she was going to be extremely satisfying tonight. Then, as soon as they were back in Chicago to catch their plane to the coast, Sarah would manage to lure him into a costly shopping safari through all the Michigan Avenue snob shops.

By the time McNeill reached his motel room, he was feeling quite happy. Realizing what was at stake had made him all the more determined to win. And he would win. He knew that now. He'd call Silas Camp in the morning, get his approval, and then start to work.

CHAPTER V

Brennan muttered angrily and rattled the glass door on the newspaper stand. He'd deposited his fifteen cents, but the damn gate wouldn't budge. He searched his pockets, deposited another nickel and dime, and tried again to obtain a morning copy of the **Tribune.** He might just as well have attempted to penetrate Fort Knox.

Brennan looked about the lobby hoping to see someone who could help him, but nobody seemed to give a damn. He shrugged and resolutely entered the coffee shop. He paused inside the restaurant and waited for the hostess, just as the sign commanded. The hostess, a well-girdled, heavily made-up matron, was, however, involved in a conversation with the truck driver seated at the counter. Brennan finally gave up and sat down at the nearest empty table.

"Your order?"

Brennan shifted his glance to the coffee-stained and totally uninteresting bosom of his waitress. "Could I have a menu?"

"Supposed to get that from Mildred," she muttered.

After a heated exchange between Mildred and Brennan's waitress, the latter returned with a menu. Brennan opened the folder, scanned it quickly, and ordered juice, country scrambled eggs, crisp bacon, and black coffee.

He lit a cigarette and let his thoughts drift to one of his favorite subjects—good food. Breakfast invariably reminded him of that delightful French restaurant on Royal street in New Orleans. He fancied they'd named the place after him.

59

Ah, to start this day with an icy Pernod, then Oeufs Hussarde. Brennan was remembering the winy tang of the Marchand de Vin sauce when the waitress returned with his order. He glanced down at the watery eggs, the limp bacon, the greasy toast and involuntarily grimaced.

"Enjoy," said the waitress as she departed.

"Thanks," Brennan replied with a distinct lack of enthusiasm.

McNeill, still in his motel room this time of morning, recited his credit-card number to the operator, then asked for Silas Camp's unlisted number in Texas. After a ring and a half, his boss picked up the phone.

"Lawrence McNeill here, Mr. Camp."

"Where are you, McNeill?" the crusty old voice demanded.

"Place called Rossdale, Illinois, Mr. Camp. Followed Dr. Brennan up here."

"What's that quack doing there?"

"Says he's here on some child battering thing. A murder trial. Nothing connected with us."

"Don't suppose we're lucky enough for Brennan to be personally involved in the killing?" Camp asked hopefully.

"No, damn it."

"Then it's trouble with the doctor, is it?" Camp hissed.

"I'm afraid it is," McNeill replied. "He's one hardheaded son of a bitch. Couldn't budge him."

"We can budge anyone, McNeill." Camp's voice became emphatic, full of confidence. "If we have to."

"He tells me he's supposed to testify before Senator Black's committee in a few weeks," McNeill added. "About us."

"Is Black up for re-election this year?"

"No sir. He has four more years to go on this term."

"Damn. Senators are always more reasonable during their re-election years.

"What do you propose, McNeill?" Camp asked as an after-thought.

"Brennan seems to be chronically unhappy with his job, Mr. Camp," McNeill began. "I'd like to offer him a chance to better himself—you know what I mean?"

"Think it'll work?"

McNeill was convinced that his plan would work, so he did not hesitate to sell it to his boss. "Yes, Mr. Camp, I think Dr. Brennan will see the light. I think he'll opt for the good life."

"You're an optimist—as usual," Camp observed.

"Well sir, I'll certainly try my best to make this work. You know that."

"I'll expect a report on your efforts as soon as possible."

"I'll see Brennan today, Mr. Camp. Tonight at the latest."

"Call me immediately, you hear," Camp commanded.

"Yes sir."

Silas Camp's name was almost a household word. As is the norm with rich and powerful personalities, almost every-one knew something about Mr. Camp. Few knew very much. Only Silas knew it all.

The best-known thing about him was that he was a self-made billionaire. His fortune was based on vast oil holdings around the world. Having used the capital from his petroleum interests to achieve the necessary diversification, Camp was involved to some degree in most of the major industries both here and abroad.

Mr. Camp's home base was his penthouse office suite. It occupied the entire twenty-sixth floor of the Camp Petroleum Building in downtown Houston. From there Silas directed his multi-faceted business empire like an agile spider.

He was somewhere in his eighties. He rather enjoyed the endless speculation about his exact age, but he kept the secret to himself.

Camp was in reasonably good health. He prided himself on

61

his vigor and maintained a stable of physicians whose duty it was to keep him sound of body. He refrained from indulging in any vices, the single exception being his long-standing secret devotion to hard-core pornography. The doctors, the disciplined life style, and the occasional surreptitious visits to a prominent, if rather unorthodox, Swiss geriatrist maintained Silas Camp's ancient body in admirable fashion.

Mr. Camp was totally bald, had been since his early thirties. His face was that of an aged Baptist minister—pleasant, but possessing a certain intense vigor. Camp was 5 feet 6 inches tall and kept his weight at 160 pounds. He dressed conservatively, preferring standard, well-tailored business suits, white shirts, and conventional neckties to the flamboyant pseudo-cowboy attire affected by some members of the Texas aristocracy.

Despite his limited formal schooling, Silas Camp immediately impressed one with his intelligence. His voice reflected his age, but his speech was compelling and erudite. When he felt the need, he could usually sway, if not totally convert, his audience, regardless of its size.

Silas was also famous for his ability to pick the right man for any job in his vast organization. And once he had picked his man, Silas rarely lost him to the enticements of the competition. It was imperative that he have a managerial staff consisting of men who owed their total allegiance, their fortune, and in some extreme instances, even their freedom, to Silas Camp.

Such a man was Lawrence McNeill. Pembroke's vice-president was effectively owned by Silas Camp. Neither he nor McNeill entertained any doubts about that.

Years ago he'd caught Lawrence McNeill in a stupid little embezzling deal. Didn't amount to a hill of beans, except that it gave Camp a lever—the kind he liked to have over his key employees. Silas used his pry to their mutual advantage. He promoted McNeill steadily, yet constantly reminded him of his vulnerability.

It all worked out nicely. As did everything Silas touched. It was the story of his life. It was also a story that would never be completely told. Camp had safely insured this over the years.

Silas really believed he had the golden touch. From his very first effort in commerce—bartering marbles as a kid—he'd come out on top. He always knew he had this gift, this ability to turn almost nothing into a very significant something.

Early in life Silas had said goodbye to his rural midwestern heritage and headed for Texas. He got as far as Texarkana, just inside the Lone Star State, when opportunity presented itself in the form of a job as janitor in the town bank. Silas had a broom and ears. He soon began selling the information he overheard while sweeping to various oil wildcatters. They gladly paid him for inside information as to what properties the big operators were interested in. They'd rush out, lease the peripheral land, and usually end up with a tidy profit for their investment.

The young janitor soon realized his information was worth a lot more than the paltry sums the wildcatters paid him. So Silas held out for a share of the profits. And he got it.

A very few years later, young Mr. Camp, budding oil entrepreneur, bought the First Bank of Texarkana. His initial move as the new owner was to fire all the janitors and hire his own men.

Young Camp moved rapidly up the ladder of economic success. Soon he was no longer speculating in this or that oil lease, but developing whole basins of black gold. He had his failures, but they were few. His successes were frequent and spectacular. By the time he reached his third decade, his net worth in millions of dollars exceeded his age.

It was a pretax, cutthroat, survival-of-the-fittest era that spawned Silas Camp. He emerged from the quagmire as the unquestioned winner, the epitome of financial success. But it inevitably left its scars.

Silas married a quiet, mousy, little girl in 1910. He did not want or need a wife in the accepted sense of the word. Rather, he took on Cynthia as a convenient means of satiating his biological urges with the least amount of fuss and bother. She died after childbirth in 1913. Her son lived.

Silas did all the proper things of course. He buried Cynthia, then brought nurses and later tutors to his Texas mansion to raise his boy, Silas Junior.

The next years were characterized by more money-grubbing hard work. As World War I increased the demand for oil, Silas made sure he was right there to provide it—to both sides of the conflict in the beginning.

He could see the United States would soon become involved, so he began his first diversification program. By the time the United States entered the war in 1917, Silas had his operation geared to handle a lion's share of the defense needs of his country, all at a considerable profit to himself, of course.

The relationship between Silas Camp and his son during the first years of the boy's life was almost nonexistent. They both lived in the same sprawling house, but their personal contact was limited to passing in the hallways, and an occasional pat on the head.

During Junior's early school years, Silas suddenly realized this lad was the heir apparent to his empire. He'd been neglecting the boy. Junior was a valuable property. He, like all Silas's other assets, had to be developed.

As Silas saw it, the boy should be molded in the image of his father if he was to carry on. The father, who had previously been a quiet passerby in the hallway, now became an overwhelmingly demanding task-master.

Silas, Junior was a slight child who resembled his mother more than his father. He was a quiet boy, and preferred reading or sedentary activities to sports. He had no playmates, but grew up in a world totally peopled by adults. When his father began to manage his life, he accepted this as proper. But he soon began to realize that he could never hope to meet the standards his father had set up.

Junior tried. He forced himself to ride around the estate in his awkward fashion. Horsemanship was important to his father. He tried to absorb some of the too advanced knowledge his tutors threw at him. But all his efforts proved to be increasingly futile.

Silas Camp, Jr. tried very hard. Right up until his fourteenth birthday. On that day he went into his father's study, sat in his father's favorite chair, wrote a short note, and put the barrel of his father's best shotgun into his mouth.

The blood and brain spattered note read, "Father, I can't. Junior."

Silas had somebody clean up the mess and went on about his business.

The Ross County jail was situated in the basement of the courthouse. One could transact routine business in the upper stories and never really appreciate the fact that accused felons were lodged below. Patrick Brennan presented himself to a policeman who commanded a desk, a radio transmitter and receiver, a couple of telephones, and a county jail. A brightly emblazoned shoulder patch proclaimed him to be a deputy sheriff. Brennan produced his credentials and asked if he might be closeted with Jackie Teal. The officer glanced at Judge Waggoner's court order, nodded affirmatively, and led Brennan to a small office to await the arrival of the prisoner.

Brennan was replacing the legal document in his pocket when a matron escorted Jacqueline Teal into the room. She was not bad looking, though she looked older than her thirty-one years. One of those women with a pinched kind of face that after a few more birthdays would definitely connote hardness. She radiated this embryonic rigidity in her walk, her hand movements, and her overall demeanor.

"I'm Dr. Brennan. I understand you've been instructed by the court to expect my visit."

"Yes."

"Do you know why I'm here?"

"I suppose so."

She sat perfectly still and stared down at her precisely folded hands. The shapeless prison uniform gave her a somewhat asexual appearance. Her face was devoid of any meaningful expression.

"Why do you think I'm here?"

"To help me," she replied mechanically.

"Now you don't really believe I'm here to help you, do you?"

This inspired a momentary speculative flicker of her eyes. But she said nothing.

"Why are you here in this jail, Mrs. Teal?"

"Because my little girl died."

"Come now. Lots of children die, but their parents don't all end up in jail. Why are you here—really?"

"You know why."

"No. You tell me. Why?"

"They said I hurt my girl. And she died. So they put me in jail."

Very rapidly, yet softly, Brennan volleyed the next question. "Who is they?"

"Moth—The police!"

"Who?"

"The police. The cops. The goddamn law. Who the hell you think runs this jail?" Her previously dull eyes were flashing now. The hint of hardness in her face had turned to granite.

"Okay, Mrs. Teal. You answered my question." This woman's hostility was barely submerged and easily provoked. Brennan was not surprised. He had found a short-fused temper to be a common trait among child abusers.

"I suppose you'll want to know all about my sex life now.

Like those other headshrinkers did. Well, let's see. I was lily-pure until my wedding night, when that beast I married tried to —"

"I'm not a psychiatrist, Mrs. Teal."

"Yeah. Well, this rapist—you're not?"

"No."

"What kind of doctor are you?"

"I'm a pediatrician."

"A pediatrician? Don't you think you're a little late?"

"I hope not, Mrs. Teal. I'm here to try to understand you—and what you did to Helen, and why. And then I'll report back to the court and try to get the judge to understand."

"You won't understand. Neither will the judge or anyone else."

"Try me."

"Why should I?"

"What have you got to lose?"

"Eh?"

"I said what have you got to lose. You pleaded guilty to murder. You know what they can do to you already. So what more can I do?"

"You gonna help me?"

"I don't know if I can. I don't know whether I'll understand you or not."

"Oh, now I get it. I open up to you, then you twist it around so they can all feel self-righteous and hang me. Then every-body goes home and sleeps real good. Except me."

"Look, Mrs. Teal," Brennan said. "Who told you I was going to come and see you?"

"The judge."

"Did your lawyer—Do you trust your lawyer?"

"Sometimes. He tries."

"Did he say whether you should talk to me or not?"

"He said it was okay to talk to you. You know, you and the other doctors are the only ones Mr. Delaney ever let me talk to. He was madder than hell when he found out I'd talked to the police right after the—right after Helen died."

"Now, Mrs. Teal, I can't make any promises to you, but I would like to hear your version of what happened. Only if you want to tell me, of course."

"Well—"

"Look, Mrs. Teal. You call your attorney and tell him what I've said. Then ask what you should do."

"Well, I did hear the judge say I should cooperate with the new doctor."

"Yes, Mrs. Teal. But you do not have to incriminate yourself to me or to anyone else. You'd better check with Mr. Delaney. Tell him I want to talk with him myself. He can call me at the motel. Then, if everyone agrees, I'll be back to see you."

Patrick Brennan left the jail and immediately took the elevator to the third floor of the courthouse. He requested a brief audience with Judge Waggoner, and was immediately shown into his chambers.

"Good morning, Doctor. How are you?"

"I have a problem that I hope you can help me with."

"Well, I'll certainly try. Sit down, make yourself comfortable, and tell me about it."

"I just had a chat with Mrs. Teal. The question arose as to just how candid she can or should be with me. Let me explain."

"By all means."

"Well, Your Honor, I got the idea that—No, that isn't exactly right. I got the feeling that Mrs. Teal was trying to make a deal. She talks, and I return it to you as a plea for leniency, or I set everything up for an appeal.

"I mean, I assumed that there was no privileged doctor-patient relationship here. But if Mrs. Teal tells me something important, can I talk about it in court? I guess I just got scared, Judge. So I ended the interview, and here I am."

"Well let's take a look at the whole situation. Now you are an amicus curiae. A friend of the court. In this case you're not advising the court on a question of guilt or innocence. The defendant has already pleaded guilty to the murder. And you are not furnishing information on the law concerning this murder. Those issues are settled.

"You're here to help the court understand why this admittedly guilty mother killed her infant. And I asked you here to do this. That in itself might put your value to the court in jeopardy, particularly since this is a criminal case. I thought of that. So I asked both the prosecution and the defense to agree to my bringing you here as an advisor. And both did.

"I'm not the Supreme Court, but I think I've covered all the bases, particularly in a hearing limited to mitigation and aggravation. I think we—you—are on solid legal ground in this case. I understand your worry, but I think it will be all right.

"I gave all this a lot of thought before I ever contacted you, so this court will uphold your expert witness role in this case. And I think any court of appeal will agree. As far as I'm con-- cerned, you can ask Mrs. Teal whatever you like."

CHAPTER VI

It was a quiet little street, the houses not new, but generally well kept. Brennan parked his car in front of the one home that was obviously vacant. The window shades were down, the glass in the front storm door was broken, and a decrepit auto was sitting in the drive. The faded numbers above the doorway confirmed Brennan's hunch that this was the Teal residence. It already had that certain patina of disuse a house acquires when it no longer functions as a home.

Nobody responded to the physician's knock at the house to the left of the Teals'. To the right, an elderly woman had the door open before he reached the front step. Brennan introduced himself and promptly learned that this nosy neighbor was Mrs. Alsop.

Brennan was not surprised to find that she was more than willing to discuss the Teal case. He accepted her invitation to have a cup of coffee and went inside.

"Never had nothing like this in the neighborhood before, Doctor. Who'd have thought it. A murder. And right next door. What kind of doctor are you? An M.D.?"

"Yes I am, Mrs. Alsop."

"You one of them Chicago alienists?"

"No, ma'am. I'm not an analyst; I'm a child specialist."

"Good. I guess that means, you ain't here to help that Teal bitch, huh? Pardon me. I don't ordinarily use that sort of language. Anyway, she don't deserve no help."

"I'm afraid Mrs. Teal is past any help from me, Mrs. Alsop."

"She sure is. Kid-killer! Right next door. If only I had known what was going on in that place. If—"

"Did you ever see or hear anything that would indicate to you that Mrs. Teal was mistreating her children? Particularly little Helen."

"Lord sakes, no. She kept that place shut up just like it is now. Afraid to let the sun shine in on her filthy sins. Why, if I'd had any idea she was slowly killin' that baby, I'd have called the law. But the way she kept herself and those kids locked up in that house, nobody knew what she was up to."

"Wasn't very neighborly, eh?"

"No sir."

"How long did the Teals live there?"

"Oh, at least a year. When they first arrived I tried to be friendly. Took over some coffee for a chat. You know—that sort of thing. But she didn't want any friends. Acted real funny—like she was scared of me or something.

"Oh, she was polite enough. But she acted like she was in a shell or something. Mind you, I tried to be friendly, and some of the other ladies around here tried too. But nobody could get anywhere with that cold fish. So we just quit."

"No one really knew her?"

"Not that I know of. 'Cept her husband. And she finally drove him out. A real loner, that Teal woman."

"Ever notice anything peculiar about the kids? What I mean, Mrs. Alsop, is did you notice any bruises on little Helen? Or anything out of the ordinary?"

"Not much, Doctor. But I do recollect seeing that poor child limping around the back yard last summer. God help me, if I'd only known what it meant. I just thought she'd fell and hurt herself. If only I'd guessed what was really going on, and right under my nose, I'd have reported it, and maybe she'd be alive today.

"I gotta admit, Doctor, it just never did occur to me that she was beatin' that baby all the time. Especially the way that older girl—what's her name—ah, Monica. Especially the way that Monica acted."

"What did you notice about Monica, Mrs. Alsop?"

"Well sir, the few times I was in that place, that little Monica was a perfect angel. When they moved in, she was just a little over three years old. That's when I was still trying to be neighborly. I'd go over there and Monica would take my sweater and hang it up. She'd get out the coffee things and serve. Even pour the hot coffee. Never spilt a drop. She'd wait on me hand and foot, Dr. Brennan. I just never did see anything like it in a three-year-old child. She was a real little lady."

"That's not a child you just described. Not a normal preschool child, at any rate. That's a servant. And the reason Monica acted that way is simply because she had to. Mrs. Teal offered her children no alternatives. They had to live according to her rules or else. One of the girls accommodated herself to the rules and survived. The younger one didn't."

Brennan thanked Mrs. Alsop and walked back to the Teal house. He wanted to examine the place and neighborhood a little more carefully.

He made his way past the dying auto to the fading white board fence that enclosed the back yard. The tall bushes that grew beside the fence effectively screened out both next-door neighbors' view of the Teals' back yard. The back of the lot presented a relatively open vista, however. The plank fence ended at a higher, chain-link fence belonging to the house directly behind the Teals'. There was no alley. Whoever lived in that place, Brennan reasoned, would have had the best chance to observe what went on in the Teal yard.

The contrast between the bare Teal yard and the yard opposite, with its bright-colored swings and sandbox, was painfully sharp. Brennan envisioned Monica and Helen peering through the wire fence, watching their contemporaries swinging, or building sand castles, or just doing what kids are supposed to do when they play outside. So the Teal girls were in one sense fenced in, but in another sad way, very effectively fenced out of the happy world in which children rightfully belong.

With this thought still in mind, Brennan got into his car and drove around the block to the home he now had to visit. He rang the doorbell and was promptly greeted by an attractive young matron.

"Pardon me. I'm Dr. Brennan. Mrs.—?"

"Clarkson." She automatically wiped her hand across her apron and brushed a stray lock of hair back into place. "Mrs. Clarkson."

"Wonder if I can talk with you for a few minutes, Mrs. Clarkson? About the Teals."

"Oh." She thought about his request, then shook her head. "The Teals. No. No, I don't want to talk about them." She started to close the door, nervously shifting her previously friendly eyes away from Brennan's.

"Just a moment, Mrs. Clarkson." As he spoke, he fleetingly entertained the idea of putting his foot in the door. Fortunately, Mrs. Clarkson made this embarrassing gesture unnecessary. "I have a court order," Brennan added quickly. He reached into his inside coat pocket and extracted the bulky legal papers. "If you won't talk with me here, I'm afraid I'll have to compel you to come into court Friday and tell what you know at the open hearing. And with some pretty sharp lawyers asking the questions instead of me."

"Oh well, come on in, Dr.—what did you say your name was?"

"Brennan. Dr. Patrick Brennan," he replied as he followed her into her living room.

"Take your coat, Doctor?"

"Thank you. Just throw it over a chair."

Ignoring his advice, she carefully hung his topcoat in an entry closet, then returned and sat primly in a chair opposite her guest. "I was afraid I'd get involved in that mess," she sighed. "I hoped, after all these months, maybe I'd made it. But I'm not surprised you're finally here."

"What can you tell me about the Teals, Mrs. Clarkson?"

"I hardly knew her at all," she answered. "Just passed a few words with her on the rare occasion we both happened to be out in our yards. If Mrs. Teal was in a civil mood, that is."

"I guessed it would be like that. I also guessed that you saw a great deal more of what went on behind the Teal house than anybody else. Right?"

Mrs. Clarkson looked down at her hands. "Yes. You're right, Dr. Brennan. I did see some things." She sighed, then looked directly at her guest. "I couldn't believe my eyes, Doctor. Oh, how often I've prayed I'd never witnessed it!"

"What did you see, Mrs. Clarkson?"

"About what you'd guess. I suppose I saw a murderess learning her trade," she said melodramatically. "I saw just about every kind of slapping and beating and whipping you can imagine, Doctor. Not just once or twice. It was a routine thing over there.

"I used to be glad when the weather was bad. At least I knew that Teal woman would keep her brutality indoors."

"That bad, was it?" Brennan asked, his voice conveying sympathy he did not feel.

"It was horrible. I was afraid to let my children play in their own back yard. Can you imagine such a situation? Not that Mrs. Teal would have abused mine. I just wanted to spare them the sight of her brutality. It would make you sick, some of the things she did."

"What sort of things, for instance?"

"Do I have to? I hate to even think about it."

"It'll help me a lot, Mrs. Clarkson. Just an example or two?"

"Oh, all right," she sighed. "Let's see." The young lady

rested her chin on her hand and sat looking pensive for a moment. "One of the saddest things was just to see little what's-her-name, the dead one?"

"Helen," Brennan offered.

"Yes. To see poor little Helen always limping around the yard. Or not using one or the other arm. She was always covered with bruises and cuts and things."

"When did you first notice this condition?"

"Soon as they moved in. I can't remember the baby any other way. What's the word you doctors use for these cases?" She paused, then added with a happy smile, "Battered. That's it. Helen appeared to be perpetually battered."

Dr. Brennan was finding it increasingly difficult to maintain an objective attitude toward the woman. "How about specific episodes of abuse, Mrs. Clarkson?"

"The worst I can remember was last July. My husband Clifford and I were sitting in our little screened-in veranda out back. It was that time of evening when the light is fading but you can still see things very clearly.

"We were just sitting there talking quietly when we saw Mrs. Teal and Helen come out of their back door.

"Mrs. Teal strolled around the yard, smoking a cigarette. Helen limped along behind her, stopping every now and then to pick up something or other. After several minutes, Mrs. Teal called Helen to her.

"The little girl ran to her, just as any two-year-old would. Mrs. Teal knelt down and took Helen into her arms."

She stopped her story at this point and shook her head at Brennan. "You're not going to believe this, Doctor, but it happened. Cliff and I saw it."

"What did you see?" Brennan asked impatiently.

"That woman, that so-called mother, you know what she did to that child?"

"No."

"She stood up, holding Helen with only her left arm. Then

76

she calmly took the cigarette out of her mouth, raised up the little girl's dress, and ground the cigarette out into the small of her back."

Brennan stared at her in horror.

"Told you you wouldn't believe it," Mrs. Clarkson added smugly.

"You saw this happen? You and your husband?"

"We sure did, Doctor."

"In July of last year?"

"Yes."

"What did the two of you do about it?"

"Well, we were sickened and disgusted, naturally."

"But what did you do about it?" Brennan asked in a louder voice.

"Do?"

"Yes. Do!"

Clasping her hands in exasperation, she confided, "You don't understand, Dr. Brennan."

"What don't I understand, Mrs. Clarkson?"

"I have my children to think about. I tried to explain that to you before but—"

"I understand that," Brennan interrupted coldly.

"Then there's my husband," Mrs. Clarkson went on hurriedly, defensively. "He's the alderman for this ward and it was an election year. A man in his position can't afford—"

"I see. So you did nothing?"

"We discussed it, of course. But what could we do about it? Now, really, Doctor, what could we—"

"You could easily have saved a beautiful little girl's life, Mrs. Clarkson." Brennan was no longer angry—just tired and very disgusted. "That's what you could have done last July."

Later that afternoon Patrick Brennan sat in the easy chair in his motel room, poring over the psychiatrists' report on

Mrs. Jacqueline Teal. The psychiatrists had interviewed Jackie's parents in depth. They had found them to be very rigid and strict. They were highly critical of their daughter in general, and were absolutely horrified by the fact that she had murdered their grandchild. How dare she do this to them! Not primarily upset about what she had done to Helen, but rather about how the crime affected them.

They couldn't understand it. They insisted that they had raised their Jacqueline differently. They had demanded obedience and submission from her, just as they did from her brother. None of that modern permissive nonsense during Jackie's formative years. No close relationship between parent and daughter. She—Jackie—damn well knew her place in those days.

Reading the report, one simple fact became obvious to Brennan, just as it has become obvious to the other doctors. Jackie Teal had been raised in a puritanical icebox instead of a home. So when she found herself in the role of a parent, she naturally called upon her previous experiences. These were her sole guidelines in regard to family relations, so she applied what she knew to her own house, her own children. But she had learned her lessons too well. She over-applied the obedience and the submissiveness, and when it came to discipline, she lost her head.

The psychiatrists stated that Mrs. Teal had been exposed to very little love in her formative years. Her childhood was oriented solely toward the rights and privileges of her parents. Her personal needs, if considered at all, had been unimportant.

The doctors concluded that Jacqueline entered her adult life with an intense need to be loved—to be cuddled, protected, and cared about. But this was accompanied by her very deep-seated belief that there was no possibility or likelihood of ever really attaining such a relationship for herself.

But she had to try for a better life. So she tried marriage, hoping that it would offer happiness. James Teal, the man she chose to marry, could not provide the love Jackie needed. This was not a lack of physical love, but a deficit of tenderness and consideration of Jackie as a person—of her needs and her desires and her hopes for an independent identity. Again she had failed. And James Teal had failed. He ended his role in her life—as had all the other potential providers of love— by abandoning her.

Now, without parents, friends, or husband, Mrs. Teal had only one possible source for the empathy and understanding she longed for but had never known. Her children. And, by God, they had better deliver for her. Or else!

Brennan's thoughts were interrupted by the harsh jangling of the telephone. "Long distance calling Dr. Patrick Brennan."

"Yes."

"Is this he?"

"Yes it is."

"Go ahead, sir. Dr. Brennan is on the line."

"Delaney here, Dr. Brennan. My client called. She said you wanted to talk to me."

"Thanks, Mr. Delaney. You know what I'm trying to accomplish here in Rossdale?"

"Yes."

"Your client—Mrs. Teal—she's afraid of me."

"I know, Doctor. She's scared of me, too. She's scared to death of all outsiders. Particularly people she thinks represent authority."

"You've noticed that about her. Interesting. Tell me, Mr. Delaney, why did you plead her guilty?"

"Simple. She would've been convicted, and they would've given her the chair. So I made a deal to save her life. I'm not sure I did her any favors, but I did what I thought was best. For her. As a client."

"You don't like Jacqueline Teal very much, do you, counselor?"

"No."

"Why? Do you find her as execrable as everyone else I've talked with does?"

"I'm a lawyer. I do what I have to do, and what I think is in the best interests of my clients. Probably you do the same thing. You have to treat your patients, but you don't have to love them."

"True. Except mine are mostly lovable."

"What do you want of me, Dr. Brennan?"

"When I asked Mrs. Teal to have you call, I was afraid you might be trying to put me in a position to set up a mistrial or an appeal. Or have set up some other legal trap for me to go blundering into. But Judge Waggoner straightened me out."

"Don't underestimate me. I might have tried if I thought I had a chance. But that judge is a real old fox. It'll be a cold day before anybody puts anything over on him. When I can forget for a minute that I'm supposed to be a sharp Chicago lawyer, I admit that Judge Waggoner's the ideal man for his job. He's a real judge. Wish we had him here in the city. Damn shame he's stuck out there in the sticks."

"I agree. He's okay, the judge. I'm the one who's insecure at the moment."

" 'Fraid I can't help you."

"How about telling your client it's okay to talk to me. About the crime."

"I told her. I'll tell her again. But I wouldn't bet that it'll make any difference."

"Thanks. I'll see her again in the morning. I appreciate your call. And your efforts."

"You bet."

A few minutes later Tom Delaney was sipping a scotch and water in a bar on LaSalle Street in the heart of Chicago's legal district. The place was rapidly filling with attorneys, all planning to have a few quick drinks before heading home.

Tom—for some unknown reason everyone, friend or

stranger, invariably called him Delaney—was rather short and heavy set. He had curly, flaming red hair, a florid complexion and blue eyes. He was usually very jovial but this evening he stared soberly into his glass, thinking about his recent conversation with Judge Waggoner's amicus curiae.

Of course, Delaney had already checked on Brennan. That'd been easy. A call to Dr. Ike Cohen, the pediatrician who supervised the health of all the little Delaneys, had quickly confirmed the credentials of Patrick Brennan.

"He's a wheel, Delaney," Cohen had said. "Not too big, mind you. But a wheel. Deep in child abuse. Knows what he's doing, too. Brennan's not like a lot of pediatricians. He doesn't go around cluttering up the literature just to see his name in print. His articles are usually relevant."

"What kind of guy is he, Ike?"

"I only met him once. He and I had a few drinks together at a convention in Boston. Sat in this saloon, solved all the world's problems, you know.

"He's a tall, skinny guy. Nose like mine. Graying. A confirmed bachelor. One of those food nuts."

"Health food?" Delaney asked rather incredulously.

"Hell no," the doctor answered. "You know, a gourmet."

"You like him, Ike?"

"Yeah."

"Thanks for the information."

"Anytime, Delaney."

Delaney had to agree with Ike Cohen. Dr. Brennan sounded like the kind of guy he could get along with. Yet Delaney doubted that Brennan or anyone else could do much to help Mrs. Teal. He really wasn't sure he understood why Judge Waggoner had insisted upon bringing him into the case. The judge had just said he felt it was necessary.

For whom? Delaney had not pressed the issue, figuring his client had nothing to lose. But damn if he could see how Jackie Teal could gain anything from Brennan's belated inquiry and opinion. But, by the same token, Delaney knew Judge Waggoner was not given to idle flights of fancy in the administration of his court. He must have some very good reason for his action. And, Delaney thought, you could bet your ass the judge would make his motives crystal clear when he was damn good and ready.

God, he hated this case. In a sense, he couldn't wait till Friday. Get it over with. See the last of that Teal woman.

Hell, he had eight kids of his own. One more and he'd have enough for a sexually integrated baseball team. He'd call them the Rotenkopfers, or simply the Redheads. Why not? Sounded more apropos than Red Sox.

He looked at his watch, saw he had a half hour before his train left for Barrington, and signaled for another scotch.

It's your own damn fault, he thought. Serve as an advisor to the A.C.L.U. to salve your conscience because you have a lovely family, make a lot of money, and live in an affluent suburb far removed from the human misery that makes it all possible. So you say sure, I'll help out on a free one now and then. Always felt like a frustrated crusader anyhow. All those high-sounding motives, and you end up representing a client whose crime you deplore—a client like Mrs. Teal.

Most of Delaney's efforts on behalf of the A.C.L.U. had been a matter of preparing and filing erudite briefs on this or that alleged infringement of someone's constitutional rights. Nitty-gritty law, he often called it. Not concerned with justice, but with whether some legalistic faux pas was important enough to get a particular prisoner out of Stateville. Usually this sort of procedure had little or no relationship to guilt or innocence. It was simply the educated exploitation of legal technicalities.

Hell, it was all part of his job, Delaney thought. He paid his bar tab, slipped on his fur-collared overcoat, and headed for the station.

So he was stuck with Mrs. Teal. And he knew he had done

the right thing for her. She'd had to plead guilty, or she would've gotten the maximum. Delaney had explored every possible angle he could remotely imagine, and it still came out the same. Guilty. Premeditated. So he had talked State's Attorney Keller into a plea deal. That was the very best he could possibly do for the woman.

But God, Delaney thought, he still hated to lose a case.

Brennan returned to the psychiatric brief. He noted that the psychiatrists made mention of several personality traits that he also had noted during his one brief contact with Mrs. Teal.

She was described as immature, particularly from an emotional standpoint. She exhibited evasiveness. She was at once reluctant to talk, and then suddenly quite demanding. Often they found her quite depressed. She exhibited many psychosomatic complaints throughout the period of the interviews— migraine, nervous stomach, headaches, palpitation. She obviously found this to be a safe area in her dealings with the psychiatrists, and as the consultations progressed, Jackie increasingly avoided the painful, personal aspects of her life, substituting a discussion of various physical symptoms.

Two similar traits struck Brennan as especially significant. The doctors described Mrs. Teal as being very rigid and convinced of her rightness in all things. In addition to this strong fundamentalist streak, they felt she exhibited a marked tendency toward obsessive-compulsive behavior in relation to her environment. This trait emerged most obviously in her contacts with her children.

Brennan had to agree. This was really the crux of the whole problem. This was why Jackie Teal had killed her child. At least as far as the precipitating cause was concerned. This was what the layman had so much difficulty understanding after the fact of the crime. But Brennan was convinced that this quirk in Jackie Teal explained the attacks on her child. This was the immediate cause of the murder.

CHAPTER VII

Patrick Brennan wandered into the motel bar for a before-dinner cocktail. The evening rush had not yet begun; only a few scattered customers were in attendance.

He had finished his dreary study of the psychiatric brief and had found it disheartening, as was just about every other facet of this particular case. He was exhausted. He absently ordered his therapeutic Manhattan.

In short order the bartender appeared with his drink and literally hurled it at him. "What the hell," Brennan muttered as he jumped back to avoid being splashed. He looked up into the angry face of the night bartender. "Jerry, what—?"

"I just heard why you're hanging around here in Rossdale, Brennan, and I don't like what I heard."

"Well, little man, what was it you heard?" Brennan snapped.

The bantam bartender stretched himself to his full height of about five feet four and hissed, "I heard you're here to get that Teal bitch off free."

"That's not true, Jerry."

Jerry visibly relaxed and began wiping up the spilled drink. "I shoulda' known better, Doc. Lost my temper. Sorry."

"Okay, Jerry. I exploded too. Guess I'm tireder than I realized. I apologize."

"S'all right, Doc. We folks here in Rossdale, we're pretty upset about that case. Don't want no psalm-singin' outsiders interfering with that bitch gettin' everything she deserves."

"Well, she pleaded guilty yesterday, Jerry."

"Yeah. Sure. But you know that don't mean a hell of a lot anymore, Doc. Before long somebody'll try to make a martyr out of her. Everybody'll start feelin' sorry for her instead of for that dead kid. That's what always happens these days. And they call that justice! Shit!"

"What do you think should happen to Mrs. Teal, Jerry?"

"I know what should be done to her. But it won't. Nothing near what she deserves is gonna happen to her. Somebody oughta take that broad and slowly break all her arms and legs. Then pound her goddamn head into the floor until her eyes pop out. And beat her till there's nothin' left but a bloody pulp. 'Nother words, the same treatment for her that she gave to her own flesh and blood. Now that would be a real fittin' punishment for a change." Jerry smiled. The scene he had just described obviously pleased him.

Brennan experienced a wave of nausea. He could not help staring in abject horror at this supposedly civilized midwesterner. Without another word Brennan climbed off the barstool and stalked out of the room.

Back in his room after an ineffectual effort at dinner, Brennan felt disgusted—with people, and murderers, and lawyers, and doctors, and especially with bartenders. One of these days, as soon as he had a night he could call his own, he was going to enjoy a good old-fashioned boozing. Yes sir, saturate himself with the oldest of the tranquilizers. Then he could wake up physically ill—with dry mouth, upset stomach, and aching head—but at the same time purged of some of the tensions that now boiled and bubbled inside him.

Not knowing what to do with his hands at the moment, Brennan turned on the TV. He watched as a white dot appeared in the center of the screen, then rapidly spread into a scene depicting a pajama-clad child holding his stomach and wailing away. This was designed to convey severe illness. A very sexy mother then clasped the afflicted one to her patently man-made bosom and called, "George, bring the Gastropep. Eddie's sick." Immediately there followed a close-up of Eddie, now grinning and gratefully hugging his beautiful mommie. Then a huge bottle of Gastropep filled the screen. Out of nowhere a deep, resonant, confidence-inspiring male voice announced, "Parents, when your child gets—"

"Damn you," Brennan muttered as he snapped off the television. He lay down, lit a cigarette, and tried to relax.

Later, when Brennan was almost asleep, the phone rang. His first impulse was to ignore it, but after several rings he changed his mind. "Hello," he said impatiently.

"Lawrence McNeill, Doctor."

"Oh. Hello, Mr. McNeill. You still here?"

"Yes. The matter I discussed with you last night was only one of the reasons I wanted to see you. I couldn't say any more then, but I can now. Could you spare me just a little time this evening so we can properly finish our discussion?"

"So far my evening has been mangled by experts. Just what else did you have in mind for it?"

"What's that?"

"Nothing, Mr. McNeill. Nothing. Just come on around to my room. Be glad to talk with you."

"Certainly, Doctor. Be right there."

Patrick Brennan was surprised to find that McNeill was still in Rossdale. Somehow he'd thought the busy executive would be halfway around the world by now. But, before he could consider the reasons for McNeill's continued presence, the man was at his door.

"Had yourself a bad day, Doctor?"

"A hell of a day, Mr. McNeill. A real bitch! Wish I'd never heard of Rossdale. I came here partly seeking a diversion from my practice—something different, you know. What a joke, a very bad joke, this damn trip has turned out to be."

"You don't sound very happy with your present lot in life, Doctor."

"Oh, don't pay any attention to my grumbling. As I said, it's been a bad day."

"No. I'm very interested in your views. Particularly about your medical practice."

"It's about like any other pediatrician's, I suppose. I'm beginning to think it's a young man's business. A very young man's. I get damn tired of being called out at all hours of the night, usually to see kids that have been sick for a week. Being a slave to the telephone gets old too. Every single conversation begins exactly the same way—'I'm sorry to disturb you, Doctor, but—' The hell they're sorry! No physician objects to genuine emergency calls. At any hour. But most of these parents will sit and smile at a sick kid all day. It only becomes urgent when the kid disturbs his mommy and daddy's sleep. Then they just have to share this delightful experience with me. So I work myself to death and end up nowhere.

"And God, the stupidity of some parents. You just wouldn't believe it, Mr. McNeill. You wouldn't believe it."

"You sound bitter, Dr. Brennan."

"Yeah, I know I do. Guess I am. Seems like the fun has gone out of it. I sort of feel my life has just been a series of honorable mentions.

"It's a disturbing thing, you know, to be past forty and then find yourself plagued with doubts as to whether or not you picked the right role for yourself." Brennan was silent now, slightly embarrassed by the dismal monologue he had found himself pouring out to McNeill.

"It's not too late for a change, Doctor," McNeill said softly.

For a moment this quiet remark seemed to escape the physician's notice. Then he began to realize what McNeill had said. "What? What did you say?"

"I said it's not too late for the good life, Doctor. It can still be yours."

88

"What's that supposed to mean?"

"That's the other thing I wanted to discuss with you. Last night I had two purposes in mind. One we discussed at some length, as I'm sure you remember. The other was to look you over. An expedition of appraisal, you might say."

"Why?"

"Since the beginning of your rather enigmatic relationship with our company, we've had occasion to check you out pretty thoroughly, Doctor. And I'm glad to say that you check out very well—honest, sincere, dedicated, a man of honor. Respected by your colleagues. And by your patients, too. Lots of flattering adjectives have consistently appeared in our reports on you, Dr. Brennan. Having met you, I'm sure that our reports were correct, that you were not misrepresented to the company."

"You make me sound like a paragon of virtue, Mr. McNeill. And I still wonder why."

"For some time now Pembroke Drugs has felt the need for a medical director. It has occurred to us that a man of your training and experience would fulfill our needs quite admirably."

Brennan wondered if he could possibly look as wide-eyed as he felt at this moment. "Let me get this straight, Mr. McNeill. You're offering me a job? With Pembroke Drugs?"

"Not just a job, Dr. Brennan. A top executive post with a large manufacturer of proprietary medications. I can promise you beautiful working conditions. Enough travel to make it interesting. A top salary. Stock options. Almost a sure crack at any vacancies that might come up on our board of directors. In short, I'm offering you a new life. Starting at the top."

"You're really serious?"

"Damn right, I'm serious. And you should be equally serious. Think of it—no more calls at all hours, no more nagging parents, no more of any of those things you enumerated as typical of your present existence. A new life!"

Patrick Brennan slowly stood up and began thoughtfully pacing up and down. He was silent for a long while. Then he sighed and sat down again. After a long silence, he looked directly at McNeill and said, "Just one question. What are you people going to do about the salol in the Gastropep formula?"

"That is an entirely different subject, Dr. Brennan. We pretty well exhausted it last evening. Now I'm interested in your reaction to my offer."

"Well, I guess that answers my question. Tell me this, please. What is the difference between your proffered top executive post and an ordinary bribe?"

"What?"

"A bribe," Brennan quietly repeated.

"Well now. Well, I never heard of such a—"

"Relax, Mr. McNeill. I'll ask the question again. What is the difference?"

"I think you're being rude, Doctor."

"I'm sorry. Don't mean to be. But I am curious to see if you can pretend that your job offer is anything other than a flagrant attempt to get me to lay off your damn Gastropep. Can you?"

"You're taking a very narrow and silly stand on this, Brennan. And a potentially dangerous one."

"Now, that almost sounds like a threat."

"We're a big and powerful company, Doctor. And you don't get to be big or powerful by being a flaming idealist. You get to the top by being hard and practical and tough when you have to be. And when you are at the top, you protect your position. It isn't always pleasant, but it's essential to the survival of a great corporation."

"I see. The end justifies the means. That one is always raising its ugly head." Brennan was still scrutinizing the executive intently. "Care to spell it out in detail? I mean just what you've got in mind to bring me around to your way of thinking?"

"I take it you're not interested in a position with Pembroke Drugs," McNeill said coldly.

"That is correct, Mr. McNeill. I may not be very happy or very bright. But I sure as hell am not reduced to selling my soul to you or your damnable company."

"Well, I'm sorry. I thought I was dealing with a responsible and reasonable man. I was wrong. Good-bye, Dr. Brennan."

Just as he reached the door, Brennan arrested his momentum with a final observation. "Just one more thing, Mr. McNeill. I have no idea what sort of revenge you're conjuring up for me, but forget it. Save us both a lot of time and trouble."

McNeill glared back at the physician, who now seemed very relaxed and confident. McNeill started to say something, but apparently thought better of it and slammed the door with a resounding crash.

CHAPTER VIII

Three police agencies were responsible for law enforcement in the Ross County area.

The Illinois State Police devoted most of their time and effort to patrolling the state and federal highways of the county. There was an investigative arm of the state department, but they rarely operated in or around the Rossdale area. Occasionally, in late summer, an undercover agent or two attempted to infiltrate the eager group of wholesalers intent on harvesting the marijuana crop that grew wild in the area.

Ross County also had a sheriff, as did every other county in Illinois. He was an elected official who served a four-year term. Those who dispensed political patronage considered the sheriff's office and his deputy jobs to be among the real plums of a local election. In a one-party county, a degree of experience and expertise could have evolved over the years. In Ross County, however, the sheriff's office kept seesawing back and forth between the two major parties. This situation made it impossible to maintain any degree of job security or professionalism within the sheriff's office. The sheriff watched over the rural regions of the county, ran the county jail, and provided guards and bailiffs for the courts.

The city of Rossdale maintained its own police force consisting of twenty men under the direction of Captain Grant Miller. At one time there had been a chief of police in Rossdale. After his death, the then-mayor had offered the title to Captain Miller.

93

Grant thought about it, then frankly discussed the matter with Mayor Richard Douglas. "Don't think I want the chief's title, Dick. But I would like to stay captain and still have the job."

"That doesn't make any sense, Grant."

"Sure it does. Think about it."

"What's to think?" the mayor countered.

"Well," Miller began, "all I get if I take this promotion is the title 'Chief of Police'. Pay's practically the same as my captain's salary. And if I take it, I lose my civil service status. So, in a few years along comes another mayor of a different party and I'm out on my ass.

"If I stay captain, and you don't appoint somebody else as chief, I'm way ahead. I get the job and retain my professional standing. The worst that can happen is some future mayor will appoint a political hack as chief. I've lived with them before and I can do it again."

"Makes sense," Mayor Douglas agreed.

Grant Miller was now serving under his third mayor since Dick Douglas. He still had the title of captain, and most citizens had long since forgotten that the job of police chief had ever existed in Rossdale.

Miller was fifty-three years old. He'd been a policeman almost all his adult life. He'd started as an MP in the Army during World War II, and had become a patrolman with the Rossdale force after the war.

He liked his job and worked hard at it. He had finagled his way into every school or course he could, and as his knowledge and experience increased, he had moved steadily up through the ranks to the top. He could have retired with twenty years service six years ago, but the idea did not seem to Miller to be worth serious consideration. Larger police departments had tried to lure him out of Rossdale, but he never gave these offers much thought either. Miller liked Rossdale. He felt that the place had been good to him and that he owed the town the benefit of his police acumen, since Rossdale had made it possible for him to get it in the first place.

Grant Miller and his wife, Anita lived in a Cape Cod style house in a comfortable neighborhood on the west side of Rossdale. Their only child, Cynthia, now lived in Colorado with her husband, who was a successful young attorney, and their two children. She had recently told the Millers that they could expect their third grandchild in the spring.

This wintery Tuesday evening the Millers were sitting in front of the fireplace with their after-dinner coffee. Grant took his shoes off and propped his feet on the hearth.

After several minutes of silence, Anita put aside the evening paper and looked at her husband. He was staring into the fire as if hypnotized by it. "Do you want to tell me what's bothering you, Grant? I know you, and you're not bright enough to solve it by yourself, so you may as well tell me now."

"Shut up, old woman. Can't you see I'm thinking?" he affectionately replied.

"Old!" she expostulated, feigning an expression of shock.

"Well, maybe not too old yet," he laughed and placed his hand on her knee. "Get some more coffee and I'll consider telling you."

When Anita returned with the coffee, Grant sighed and said, "I guess it's the Teal case. Or rather that damn Dr. Brennan."

"Why damn Dr. Brennan?"

"I don't know." Grant moved his feet away from the fireplace and continued. "He's probably a pretty nice guy. Wish I'd met him under different circumstances."

"Grant, you know better than to allow your personal feelings to get snarled up in one of your cases. Why'd you let this Teal case get to you?"

"I know," Grant replied. "How well I know."

"Well, why did you?"

"The little kid was bad enough, Anita. But that mother,

that Mrs. Teal. You wouldn't believe a woman like her could exist." He got up, began to pace about the small room. "I couldn't begin to tell you about her. Hell, I've seen just about every kind of killer or felon there is, but believe me, I never saw anything like this cold fish. She tortures her baby to death, then she's upset because she died so soon. Helen Teal was supposed to live a little longer. Her mamma wasn't ready to give her up yet."

"What has that got to do with Dr. Brennan?" his wife asked.

"Don't know," he answered. "Probably nothing. It's just that I know this case. I know how I feel about it. And I don't know how, if any way, Brennan is going to be able to influence the judge."

"Now Grant," she admonished, "you know Judge Waggoner is a good man. I've heard you sing his praises for years. Why worry about that?"

Grant sat down and picked up his coffee. "You're right, Anita. I mean when you said I let my emotions get ahead of me in this case, you hit the nail on the head. But let me ask you this. How the hell do you untangle yourself once you're snared?"

Anita walked behind his chair, took his head affectionately in both her hands, and kissed his wrinkled forehead. "I don't know, Grant. But I do know you. So I'm not going to worry about it. You'll do what's right in the end." She kissed his brow again. "I haven't the slightest doubt about that."

Grant started to reach for her hand, but the telephone rang. He shrugged and reached for the phone. "Hello."

"Captain Miller?"

"Yes."

"Dr. Brennan."

"How nice, Doctor. What do you want?"

"You know an alderman named Clifford Clarkson?" Brennan asked.

"Sure," Grant answered.

96

"You know he lives right behind the house Jim Teal and his wife rented?"

"Yeah," Grant said. "So what?"

"Did you question him after Helen Teal was killed?"

"No."

"Why not?"

" 'Cause he came to me about it."

"You didn't mention him to me, Miller. Nor did I see any report on his statement in your voluminous file."

"Probably because there is no report from Clarkson in the file," Miller answered sarcastically.

"What did Mr. Clarkson say to you about the Teal case?"

Miller very patiently replied, "Nothing. He said he and his wife knew nothing, saw nothing, heard nothing. They were sorry. Both wished they could help me out."

"And you believed them?" Brennan asked.

"Why not?"

"The alderman lied to you, Miller. He and his darling wife both—"

"You gotta be careful about who you go around calling liars, Doc. That careless habit could get you in trouble."

"Oh, I see," Brennan observed. "How could I have been so naive."

"Now just what the hell is that supposed to mean, Dr. Brennan?" It was Anita Miller asking the question. She had picked up the extension phone in the bedroom.

"Get off the phone, Anita," Miller snapped.

"Shut up, Grant. Dr. Brennan, are you implying that my husband is covering up some stink for Clarkson? If that's what you mean, say it."

"I'm not going to battle with your wife, Miller. Goodnight," the doctor said quietly.

"Wait a minute. Just a goddamn minute please," Miller said loudly. "Now, I don't know what you want, Doc. I told you the truth. Clarkson came to me the day after Helen was killed. He said he surmised we might be asking them some questions because they lived close to the Teals. He said he wanted to spare me the trouble. They didn't know the Teals so they could add nothing to the case.

"Hell, I had Mrs. Teal's confession in hand before that. I had no reason to question the man's good intentions."

"That means you dropped it as far as the Clarksons were concerned?" Brennan asked.

After a pause, the policeman reluctantly said, "Yes."

"Captain Miller," Brennan said in a very controlled voice. "And Mrs. Miller—are you still there?"

"Yes."

"The Clarksons had a very pleasant summer. They sat comfortably on their screened-in veranda—keeps the bothersome mosquitos out, you know. Anyway, they sat there and casually observed Mrs. Teal systematically killing her little girl, Helen. Not just once, mind you. They enjoyed this scene all summer long."

"Oh shit," Grant mumbled.

"No, Captain, it's true. They both sat there on their uninvolved asses and watched Jackie Teal get the job done on little Helen. All summer long."

Grant Miller now held the telephone as if it were his one connection with reality. "They say why, Dr. Brennan?" he asked almost inaudibly.

"Yes, Captain Miller, she—Mrs. Clarkson—did. She said they didn't want to get involved. They didn't want their children exposed to the situation any more' than necessary. And, as she reminded me, an alderman can't afford to get involved in messy things like that—especially during an election year."

CHAPTER IX

Wednesday morning was cold but sunny, a welcome change from the gray monotony of the past several days. Brennan felt well rested and mentally refreshed as he stood on the steps of the Ross County Courthouse. He seemed reluctant to leave the radiant sunlight for the predictable gloom of the jail.

Remarkable how his outlook on life had improved since the night before. Yesterday had been a real bitch. But the final unpleasant confrontation with McNeill, which could have been the coup de grace, had actually had a cathartic effect on the doctor. Mr. McNeill had confirmed his worst suspicions about Pembroke Drugs with his shabby attempt at bribery. After that he felt better, slept soundly, and awoke refreshed and ready to plunge back into the entangle- ments of the Teal case.

Brennan noticed that the prisoner seemed to be a little calmer this morning. "Good morning," he said. "It's a brighter day today."

"Yes."

"You chat with your lawyer? About me?"

"Yes. He said I could trust you. Said I should cooperate."

"Good. Now, I'm supposed to get to know you, Mrs. Teal, as I said yesterday, so I can explain you to the court. Particularly in regard to your relationship with your chil- dren. More specifically about what happened to Helen."

Brennan could see that this was still a touchy subject. She became fidgety and looked away from him.

"No, Mrs. Teal. That won't do. If I am to be of any value to anybody here, you and I have to communicate. Now I know what happened to Helen. So do you. It happened. Our talking about it won't undo it or make it worse. I know it's painful for you. However, I am probably the safest confidant you're going to find. Understand what I'm trying to say?"

"Yes. I think I do."

"Okay. Let's get at it. You can quit—tell me to go to hell—anytime you want. You're still free in that regard. Okay?"

"Okay."

"Why did your husband move away last summer?"

"We just couldn't get along. Really surprised me we didn't break up before."

"Must have been sort of tough on you, Mrs. Teal. I mean being left alone with those kids to take care of." Brennan was trying to get the feel of the Teal house just prior to the fatal assault on Helen. He realized a direct approach would get nowhere. "How did you feel about it? Were you depressed at being deserted by Jim?"

"No. Not really. I was real upset. Very anxious. Then just plain mad."

"Mad at your husband?"

"No. Mad at everything and anything. I was sort of glad to get rid of him. But I knew it wasn't right—him taking off and all. Funny, I didn't want him back, but it was still all wrong. I could just feel how wrong everything was. And the pressure just kept building up. God, it was terrible."

Brennan nodded. He had found this to be a characteristic reaction of child abusers. They bypass depression in their response to stress. Then they rapidly or slowly build up such a head of steam that it can only be relieved by a violent reaction, usually directed toward the child whom the individual sees as being most like himself. They know they are wrong, so they punish their alter ego. That makes it right. Then they can experience normal depression. Then things are O.K. Until the insidious stress cycle begins again.

"Mrs. Teal, I want you to say the very first thing that comes into your mind when I ask you a question. The very first. Now, what comes to mind when you think back on your own childhood?"

"Children should be seen and not heard," she chanted in a childish, sing-song voice. She had obviously heard it herself—often.

"What do you take that to mean, Mrs. Teal?"

"Let's make it Jackie, Doctor. Long as you're going to probe my brain, you might as well use my first name."

"Okay, Jackie. Back to 'children should be seen and not heard.' Tell me about that."

"Oh, that was as common as good morning in my house. My folks were forever saying it—and enforcing it too. Anyway, it just popped out. Don't know—"

"What's it mean to you?"

"Well, I guess kids shouldn't interrupt or bother their parents all the time."

"You believe it?"

"Yeah. I guess so. Is that wrong?"

For the first time that morning he noted a subtle change in the modulation of her voice, a change that revealed the hostility she felt toward him as a symbol of authority.

"No. That's not wrong, Jackie." He realized it was time to change the subject. "Did you plan to have your children? I mean plan the pregancies?"

"Oh sure. The first one started in the front seat of a car at a drive-in movie. James is very athletic—a real stud." She laughed mirthlessly, then continued. "That's what I'd call

101

real family planning. Planned myself right into marriage, I did."

"And the second pregnancy?"

"I don't know. I guess I didn't really care then. Not anymore. I wasn't very happy with life, Doctor. I won't say I planned it, but I don't remember being upset about it either. Believe it or not, after I knew I was pregnant with Helen, I sort of looked forward to having her. I really did."

"Why?" Dr. Brennan asked.

"Why? Guess I sort of felt like it was another chance. For me. To be happy. I wasn't very happy—not then, not now, not ever."

Brennan was not taking notes. He didn't want to distract her in any way. He sat very quietly and asked questions only when he felt it was necessary to keep her talking, to keep the flood of vital, personal information flowing.

"What about your first baby, Jackie, I mean how did you and she get along?"

"Pretty good. Monica was a good baby. All she ever did was eat and sleep when she was little. She never much caused me any trouble. When she got older she was almost a perfect child. Very neat. And she'd always mind me. Oh, she'd catch it when she got out of line, but that wasn't very often."

"Were—are you and Monica very close? Know what I mean?"

"No. I mean yes, I know what you mean. And no, we're not what you would call real close. She's sort of a loner, plays by herself, takes care of her things, does what you tell her to."

Brennan decided to bring up the forbidden subject again. "You said you were sort of happy about having Helen. What kind of a baby was she?"

"She was something else! She was a little premature you know. God, she was an ugly kid! All wrinkled up like a little old woman. In the hospital, first time I held her, she filled her pants. Just lay there grunting and red faced and fussing. I thought then, I guess I know what this one thinks of me."

"Was she a good baby?"

"Nothing like Monica. Wanted to eat all the time. Never stopped crying. If Helen wasn't eating she was crying. I had one hell of a time trying to keep her on a feeding schedule."

"Why did you try to stick to a schedule?"

"Babies are supposed to be on a schedule. You should know that, Doctor," she said with a smile, obviously enjoying the opportunity to correct him.

"Did she have colic?"

"Yes. Terrible colic. Gassy. Yelling all the time. It got so bad once, they had to put her in the hospital. In the hospital—she was only eight weeks old then—she acted like a little angel. All she did was eat and sleep. The doctor and nurses thought I was lying about how bad she was at home. Believe me, I wasn't lying. But then I realized what the trouble was."

"What?"

"Helen didn't like me. So she fussed whenever I tried to take care of her."

"What did you do when Helen wouldn't stop crying?"

"Anything I could to keep my sanity."

"Specifically, what action did you take?"

This was the traumatic area for Jackie. Brennan could sense it in the sudden deepening of her respiration, the slight pursing of her lips.

"I'd feed her. If that didn't shut her up, I'd put her in a dark room and close the door."

"Did you ever hit her?"

"Only when she deserved it."

"Did she deserve to be hit very often, Jackie?"

"None of your damn business! She was my kid. I could

do what I liked to her." She immediately realized what she had blurted out and looked at Brennan with panic-stricken eyes. Then she buried her face in her hands and emitted a low, whimpering cry. Soon she was sobbing violently.

After a while Brennan asked in a calm, soothing voice, "Did you think you just confessed to something, Jackie? You did that with the police a long time ago. And again Monday when you pleaded guilty in court. Is that what upset you just now—another admission of your guilt?"

"Guilt. You talk about guilt," she managed to whisper between sobs. "I never meant to hurt Helen. It was an accident. I was trying to help her. To raise her right. Teach her what was right and what was wrong. I had to learn it the hard way. So did she. So it wasn't my fault. I was just doing what was right. She got hurt. She died." Now Mrs. Teal tried to focus her tear-blurred eyes on the doctor. "But just who really got it? I ask you—who? Who won? Look at me. Look what Helen did to me!"

After the abruptly aborted interview with Mrs. Teal, Brennan left the jail. He was not proud of himself or of his inquisitional methods. He realized that they had been necessary if he were to contribute anything to Friday's hearing, but he didn't have to like doing it. And he definitely did not.

As he walked out of the elevator, he was hailed by Captain Miller. "Buy you a cup of coffee, Doc?"

"Sure. Why not. Where?"

"Well, there's a machine upstairs, but the coffee's terrible. Like to stroll across the street to the cafe?"

"Fine, Captain."

A few minutes later they were sitting opposite each other in a booth, warming their hands around steaming mugs of coffee.

"How goes your social work?" the policeman asked with a distinct leer.

"Damn it, Miller, I've never seen anyone as eager to leap to conclusions as you. Let me ask you something."

"Sure."

"What are you afraid of? Is there something wrong with this Teal case that you think I might discover?"

The smirk slowly faded from the policeman's face. "No, there's nothing wrong with the Teal case. Nothing at all."

"Then why are you so opposed to my being here in Rossdale?"

"Look, Dr. Brennan, I'm a straightforward man. I'm with a clean police department in a clean town. I try to do the job the taxpayers expect. A police job. In this case that involves the brutal murder of a baby. So I work up a good investigation in cooperation with all the other officials, and it gets to court. It's so good that the defense attorney cops out and asks for a guilty plea. Up to this point everything is just fine. It's great. Then you come along. And God only knows what'll happen now."

"Well, Captain, suppose we take a look at that investigation you mentioned. I have to agree with you in part. You did an excellent job of gathering the facts about the crime. Your information is clear, concise, and meets all the requirements of the law regarding the way you can question a suspect, the rights of the suspect, et cetera. All very neat. And obviously the legal experts all agree or this case would never have progressed this far."

Brennan paused, sipped at his coffee, then said, "Well, that's what your investigation has going for it. Now, what does it lack?"

"What do you mean, lack? Hell, it doesn't lack anything that matters."

"Ah, but it does. Something that may not be important to you but obviously was important to Judge Waggoner. Even when he was handed the case all neatly tied up with a guilty plea, he still thought it was important to call in a so-called

105

expert to try to explain it all to his satisfaction. So he called me and I responded, and that's why I have the great privilege of sharing coffee with you this morning."

"Just what the hell are you talking about, Brennan?"

"Not the what, Officer. Why. That's what's missing in your really adequate investigation. And that is why I am here. The why is why."

"The what?"

"No, my friend. The why. W-H-Y. In other words, the motive for the murder. Why did Mrs. Teal act the way she did? Why did she kill her child?"

"Hell, man, I don't care why," Miller replied loudly. "I'm only interested in the fact that she did commit the murder. And I gathered the necessary evidence for a conviction. The why ain't important to me."

"Obviously, Captain. But I think it's of some importance to the judge. I'll grant you that in the course of the debate in a trial situation, the why is usually explained. But here there will be no such debate. She pleaded guilty. But the judge obviously wants this explained anyway. And he wants it explained in his courtroom, so the people of Rossdale will hear it and maybe understand it. And I sure as hell have to agree with him. Considering the sentiment in this town toward Jacqueline Teal, I'm surprised they haven't stormed the jailhouse and lynched her. Never saw such an island of hate in my life."

Brennan noted that his spiel had so far had very little effect on his companion. With scarcely suppressed exasperation, he continued to try to explain his personal role in the trial. "You and I went all over it Monday. It was horrible; it always is. I've seen children starved to death by parents who were literally upholstered in suet. And the variety of physical abuse inflicted on children would make a medieval torture master turn green with envy. I've seen burns on these youngsters from cigarettes, cigars, and radiators, from holding their hands over a burner on a stove or from dunking their hands in boiling water—all are typical of the abusive environment. Fractures, beatings, internal injuries—they run the gamut from the insignificant to the fatal.

"That's the overt side. Sometimes it's more sneaky, but the resultant mental injury can do as much if not more damage than a physical beating. One father I ran into—he worked in the stockyards—came up with the brilliant idea of taking his electric cattle-prod home with him and using it for the training and guidance of his toddler. Another made his four-year-old son watch as he boiled the child's puppy alive— to teach the lad the evils of the transgressions his father imagined he had committed."

"Sometimes, Captain, the abuse is strictly of a negative type. Here the home simply does not represent a safe haven for the baby. Poisonous drugs, toxic cleaning agents are left haphazardly lying around. Or the parents leave small children alone, with no responsible babysitter to watch over them.

"All this represents a pathological family situation of one degree or another. The term doctors like to use to describe situations like this is pathogenesis. The thing that causes the pathology. In other words, the why."

The policeman was silent. He finished his coffee, obviously anxious to terminate this unpleasant conference. Finally he said, "So that's the reason we're honored with your presence, eh, Doc? You're gonna tell us why a kid had to die. Well, good luck. I think you just might need it."

"Now wait just a minute, Captain. You ever had any courses in fingerprints?"

"Sure."

"All right. Now if you had an important case where the positive identification of a latent print would make or break it, would you get up on the witness stand and try to prove that the print was from your suspect, to the absolute exclusion of all other persons living or dead? Would you?"

"Hell no. I'd get me a fingerprint expert from the State Crime Lab."

"You would use an expert. Yet you seem quite upset because the judge wants to do the same thing. What's O.K. for you isn't O.K. for him. Is that what you're saying?"

"Look, Brennan, it's not the same thing. Not at all. If I called a fingerprint expert, I'd know what he was going to say before he ever got near the courtroom. But who the hell knows what you're going to say?"

Brennan thought about this for a minute, then said softly, "You're right. In this case, no one."

CHAPTER X

Early that sunny afternoon there occurred a brief period of congestion at the front desk of the Rossdale Motor Hotel. This was brought about by the collision of those guests checking in and those attempting to check out before the 2:00 P.M. deadline. A short queue formed at the registration desk, another at the cashier's station.

Three places back in the check-in line stood a very distinguished-looking man. He had silver-gray hair that had been professionally styled, not just cut and combed. He was of medium height, medium build. He was still reasonably young, but obviously successful—perhaps a banker, or a stockbroker. Just behind him stood a strikingly beautiful woman and a pretty blond teenager.

Finally the silver-haired gentleman reached the registration desk. "You have a reservation for me. Robert Parker. We will require two rooms, of course. One for my wife and myself and one for my daughter, Sandra. Adjacent rooms will be satisfactory."

"One moment, sir. Yes, we do have it right here. Two really lovely rooms they are. Adjacent. Just as requested. Would you register, please. And for your daughter too.

Quite some time after dinner Patrick Brennan received a phone call. He had spent several hours assembling his notes, so this interruption was almost welcome.

"Dr. Brennan?"

"Yes."

"I think maybe I should talk to you."

"Who is this?"

"My name is Teal. James Teal."

"Well—yes. I guess maybe we should talk. How long are you staying in town?"

"Leaving tonight. Don't like to hang around this place. Shouldn't even have come. Gonna leave soon as I finish talking to you. I'm here in the bar in the motel. Can you come down and meet me?"

"Yes, guess I can, Mr. Teal. Wait right there."

Brennan was surprised that James Teal had called. He thought the father had long since dealt himself out of the case.

A few minutes later Brennan walked into the bar. He glanced around, then spotted a slight, slim-shouldered man wearing a black leather jacket. He was sitting hunched up and alone at an out-of-the-way table. Brennan walked over and asked, "Mr. Teal?"

"Yeah, yeah. Sit down. You Dr. Brennan?"

"Yes."

"Call me Jim. That name of mine is just plain poison hereabouts. No point in askin' for any more trouble."

"O.K. Jim. When did you get into town?"

"Tonight. Thought I'd better come. Didn't do no good though. Saw Jackie for a few minutes. Boy, is she cold to me. Before she clammed up she said you'd want to see me. So here I am."

He was a thin-faced young man, probably in his early thirties. He had receding chin and petulant lips that partially covered widely spaced, rather prominent teeth. His eyes were small and dark, and he glanced around nervously at every sound or movement in the bar.

Brennan ordered a beer from the cocktail waitress. From his St. Louis experiences he recognized Teal's slight accent as an Ozark twang. Might be one of the transplants from the

110

hill country lured north by the attractive wages. Brennan's beer was soon delivered, along with a refill for Teal.

"I should never have left them kids with Jackie, Doc. But I thought if I really took off, maybe she'd get some sense in her head. I didn't want nothing else to happen to the girls. Guess it just made things worse—me leavin'."

"You knew Jackie was beating the children too much?"

"Yeah. Now, don't get me wrong. I don't want no spoiled young'uns. You gotta keep 'em in line. But the way Jackie'd go after 'em, specially the baby—it'd make you plain sick. She'd lean on that child all the time. Why, just before I up and left, she was smacking li'l Helen around for no reason 'tall. Helen just spilled her cereal in the highchair. Hell, kids do that all the time. But Jackie jerked her outa that chair and walloped the hell out of her. Hit her in the stomach and everything. Why, that poor baby ended up vomitin' and just wouldn't quit bawlin'. Course that just made my wife madder.

"Well, sir, I was 'fraid she'd hurt Helen bad. Somethin' inside. But she did settle down after a bit. Helen, I mean. So I just plain up and told Jackie I couldn't take no more. I packed my bag and took out for Chicago. Turns out that was just one more mistake. Seems like I can't do nothin' right."

Brennan had to agree that Jim Teal's rejection and desertion of his wife had certainly not helped matters; rather it had stimulated the final series of attacks. "Jim," he asked, "didn't you think at the time that running away was a rather poor way of handling the problem? Why didn't you go to the police, or get medical help for your wife?"

"Doc, where I come from a man don't go runnin' to the police, cause of wife trouble—unless he's a sissy. An them head doctors can't help none—'sides I can't afford 'em. I'm just a factory hand. Now don't get me wrong. I admit what I done—run off—that was bad. But 'tween you and me, I was just fed up with that woman anyhow. When I left—guess it wasn't just for the baby. It was for me too, I reckon."

"You and Jackie were busting up anyway?"

"Yeah. She wasn't really no wife to me—not no more. We was always fightin'. 'N I'd get her mad. Then she'd take it out on the kid—poor li'l Helen. She just always ended up as the goat 'tween me and Jackie. Doc, I'd play with the kids of an evenin' after supper, and that'd just make Jackie madder 'n hell. 'N sometimes Jackie'd be mad at me 'bout somethin' or other and she'd go 'n play up to baby Helen. Go all goo-goo 'n ga-ga. Hug 'n squeeze her. Hell, no wonder I thought an awful lot of the mess was 'cause of me."

"What're you going to do now, Jim?"

"Well, go back to Chicago, I guess. I got my older girl, Monica, livin' with my sister. 'Sides, I can't see how I can do no good here. Jackie don't want no part of me. And, to tell the truth, I'm plum fed up with her. Guess I just gotta try to forget. Start a new life. Don't know what else I rightly can do." He stood up and shook Brennan's hand.

"Well, thanks for stopping by to see me, Jim. So long."

Teal zipped up his leather jacket, then turned back for an instant and said, "Doc, help her if you can. She ain't all bad." Then he was gone. Brennan could understand that he'd be glad to put Rossdale, his wife, and his family tragedy behind him once and for all.

It was late now, after eleven. Brennan ordered another beer for a nightcap and thought about this latest development. Obviously there had been a great deal of hostility between the Teals. They had both tried to use the children, particularly Helen, for their own individual comfort. The baby was expected to provide solutions for her fighting parents. When she proved unable to fulfill this function, she was attacked.

Her father used the child to get back at his wife, who really needed no further provocation. And Helen had consistently failed her mother in other ways. She therefore deserved to be punished. And she was.

Brennan sipped his beer, glad he had no more company tonight. God, he was tired. This case was getting to him. Certainly was consistently depressing—like tonight.

He finished his beer and paid the tab. On the way back to his motel room, he decided to take every measure necessary to insure himself of a good night's sleep. He would close the blinds, draw the drapes, and take the phone off the hook. And he would not set his alarm clock. Finally, as a precaution against insomnia, he would read the pulp novel he'd bought in the airport until he became totally bored and exhausted. By the time Brennan reached his room, he was feeling very satisfied with his plans for the rest of the evening.

Brennan was jerked out of a somnolent haze by a loud hammering at his door. He slipped into his robe and opened the door to find a lady, fist raised, obviously prepared to continue her frantic assault on the door. "Oh Doctor, thank God," she said breathlessly.

Brennan recognized the startlingly beautiful lady. She and her family had sat at the table next to his at dinner that evening. He'd chatted with them, introductions had been exchanged, and that had been the extent of their contact. "Mrs. —Parker, isn't it?" he asked. "What can—?"

"Doctor, please help me," she pleaded, groping anxiously for his sleeve. "Come—my Sandy—it's a spasm or something. Oh, please—"

It was unexpected here, but the physician recognized the woman's panic to be the reaction of a parent to a sudden and unexpected medical emergency. "Of course, Mrs. Parker," he said reassuringly. "What is it?"

"She's all stiff and she's breathing funny." The elegantly coiffured lady now had a firm grip on Brennan's arm and was

113

literally dragging him along behind her. "We were playing bridge with another couple we met," she explained. "I'm the dummy. I just sensed I should check in on Sandy. Found her like that. What could it be, Doctor?"

"Anything like this happen before, Mrs. Parker?" Brennan asked.

"No." She opened the door of a motel room not very far from Brennan's own quarters and pushed him inside.

The doctor immediately appreciated the mother's great concern. Her daughter did indeed appear to be seriously ill. Blankets and sheets kicked aside, the young lady lay like a transfixed ballerina, her long flannel nightgown bunched immodestly about her waist. Brennan quickly scanned the girl's general appearance, simultaneously evaluating her vital signs: color good, pulse only a little rapid but strong. Breathing too fast and stridulous—an inspiratory, high-pitched crowing sound—but adequate.

One overall glance at Sandra was enough for Brennan to make a diagnosis. The agonized face—rigid, out of it, yet not quite all the way. Eyes open, staring. Body stiffened. Feet extended into the toe dancer's pose. Brennan glanced at her arms, held rigidly at her sides, and her hands—wrist bent, thumb in palm, straight fingers uncomfortably flexed at their junction with the hand.

"Mrs. Parker," Brennan said in a quiet and confident voice. "She'll be—"

"Bob—Doctor, my husband. I must get him. I'll be right back." The door slammed before Brennan could say anything more.

He shifted his attention back to the patient. She had not bitten her tongue, no involuntary urine had been passed. He tilted the bedside lamp so that the light fell across her face and was pleased to see that her pupils contracted normally.

Sandy had tetany, a syndrome which could result from any

of a number of causes. The symptoms resulted from a state of increased irritability of the muscles and nerves.

Brennan would have liked to question Mrs. Parker about the girl's medical history at this point. This being impossible for the moment, he continued his evaluation of the patient. Most likely a hysterical thing, he reasoned. Hysteria had involuntarily caused the rapid breathing with resultant loss of carbon dioxide, which had in turn caused a sudden shift in the acid-base equilibrium of the blood, and, inevitably, the neuromuscular disorder known as tetany had resulted.

Might as well give her the curative test, Brennan decided. He looked about the room and spotted a waste basket with a paper bag for a liner. He crumpled the sack to form a loose-fitting mask which he placed over the girl's nose and mouth. Rebreathing the same air time and time again slowed, then stopped, and eventually reversed the flow of carbon dioxide out of her bloodstream. It was then absorbed back into the circulation where it united with the water of the plasma to form carbonic acid, shifting the acid-base balance from the alkalotic back toward a normal ratio. This slowed the respiration and reduced the irritability of the muscles and nerves. In a matter of minutes all of the girl's distressing symptoms had disappeared. She was awake, increasingly alert and acutely embarrassed by her half-naked state.

"Feeling better now, Sandy?" Brennan asked as he helped her cover herself.

"Yes. Who are you?" she managed to ask, though obviously frightened.

"I'm Dr. Brennan. Remember, we met at dinner tonight."

"Yeah." She seemed to recognize him now. "I was so scared." Her embarrassment was very becoming, Brennan thought as he sat on the side of her bed, reassuringly holding her hand.

"Where are—?" she began.

"Your mother found you. Called me. Now she's just gone

out to get your dad," Brennan answered. "You really gave her a fright, young lady."

"I was so scared," Sandy repeated in a shivering voice. "Here in this strange room. All kinds of voices. Alone. I'm sorry. I didn't mean to—"

"That's O.K., Sandy. We all—"

"But it's all so infantile," she curtly interrupted. "Acting like a baby."

Brennan could hardly suppress a chuckle as he watched her melodramatically shield her face with her hand—a la Garbo either to hide her personal chagrin or perhaps to try and assert her imagined adulthood in her own mind as well as in his. That's all-important for kids of Sandy's age, he thought. They have to deny the child in themselves, and despite their determination to do so, their charades occasionally crumbled.

He imagined that this was just what had happened tonight. Sandy's adolescent insecurity coupled with the uncontrollable fears of a child alone at night in a strange place had precipitated the uncontrollable rapid breathing that had resulted in her hyperventilation-induced tetany.

"Try and rest now, Sandy," he ordered benignly. "I'll wait with you until your parents return. They should be along any minute now." If I had any medical paraphernalia here, I'd give her a sedative, Brennan thought. That would help prevent a repeat performance. Oh well, out here in the boondocks just have to make do with what you have."

"Thanks, Doctor," Sandy muttered sleepily. She closed her eyes and snuggled into her pillow. Apparently she felt safe now.

Actually, Brennan was rather pleased with himself. He supposed this was medical show-biz in action. You have a catastrophic-appearing illness, an accurate diagnosis, and a quick cure effected with a simple paper bag. But the ham in him had suffered. The mother had left before he'd had a chance to perform his medical magic.

Brennan wondered where Sandy's mother was now. He glanced at his wrist, saw it was bare, and then remembered he'd left his watch back in his room. He didn't know how long she'd been gone. Probably just seemed like a long time.

He quietly moved to an upholstered chair across the room. He wanted a cigarette, but he'd left those in his room too. He hoped the Parkers would return soon. He realized he was very tired.

He picked up a copy of **Seventeen** and was thumbing through the pages when something slipped out of the middle of the magazine. It was a comic book. He laughed in spite of himself and glanced at Sandy, who was sleeping soundly. How could anyone better define the thirteen-year-old female, he wondered. He carefully replaced the symbol of childhood in its hiding place.

At this point Mrs. Parker, still panic stricken, came rushing in. An equally concerned husband followed. The mother, shocked by the unexpected tranquillity of the scene, stopped short in front of her husband.

Brennan put his finger to his lips before they could say anything, pointed to the peacefully sleeping Sandra, and motioned them to follow him outside for a conference. "She's fine," he assured.

"I can't believe it." Mrs. Parker was incredulous. "Bob, she was—she looked like she—I just don't understand."

"Doctor," Mr. Parker interrupted, "is she O.K.? Jenny led me to believe Sandy was seriously ill."

"She's fine," Brennan repeated. "You folks have another room? I'm freezing."

"Oh, yes. Right next door. Come in." Mr. Parker fumbled for the key, opened the door but hesitated again. "Will Sandy be all right alone in there—I mean for a few minutes, while we talk."

117

"Sure. Let's go in," Brennan answered through chattering teeth.

"This doesn't make any sense," Jennifer Parker observed as she sat down on the nearest of the twin beds. "This is crazy. Like a bad dream. I just don't—"

The doctor stood, arms clasped across his chest, massaging himself through his thin travel robe. "Sandy had a hysterical convulsion," he explained. "Brought on, I believe, by fear of being alone at night in a strange place."

"That's ridiculous," Mr. Parker proclaimed, shaking his head so vigorously that he displaced a lock of his carefully styled silver hair. "My daughter afraid of the dark? Impossible. Why, she's been alone many times before. She won't even let us get a sitter anymore. Says that's for babies."

"She's never been an early adolescent before," Brennan countered. "They're strange people. At any rate, her fears were there tonight. And very real to her. This caused her to unconsciously begin breathing very fast—hyperventilating. It's a physical symptom, an involuntary cover-up for the irrational fear she felt."

"Rapid breathing caused all that?" Jennifer Parker's voice betrayed her skepticism.

"Indirectly, yes. This kind of respiration blows off a lot of the CO_2—carbon dioxide—from her lungs. In an attempt to maintain the necessary equilibrium, more CO_2 leaves the carbonic acid of the bloodstream and goes into the lungs, where it too is promptly blown away."

Brennan had a captive, attentive audience now. He thought perhaps this lecture would be more appropriate for medical students, but continued because he could see that the Parkers wanted to understand their daughter's sudden illness. "This causes a condition in the blood called respiratory alkalosis. This in turn leads to increased irritability of the muscles and nerves, and a rather typical kind of tonic convulsion results. It's called tetany. That's what you saw, Mrs. Parker."

"I thought you got that from stepping on a rusty nail," Bob Parker said.

"That's tetanus—an infectious disease," Brennan explained. "It too is characterized by increased neuromuscular irritability, but that and the names are about the only similarities."

"She's O.K. now?" Mrs. Parker asked. "How did you ever cure her?"

"Yeah," her husband added. "Where are your instruments and shots and things?"

"In St. Louis," Brennan answered with a laugh. "You won't believe it, but Sandra cured herself. All I did was hold the bag."

"Hold the what?"

"The paper bag," Brennan replied. "I took the paper liner out of the waste basket and held it over her nose and mouth. This caused Sandy to rebreathe all the CO_2 she was exhaling and forced it back into her lungs and into the blood. I simply reversed the flow of carbon dioxide and she cured herself."

"Well, I'll be darned," Robert Parker exclaimed.

"Will she be O.K. now, Dr. Brennan?" his wife asked.

"Sure. She's sleeping peacefully now. Too bad you weren't here to see all this. It'd be easier to understand."

"I feel so foolish," she apologized. "I was so frightened— I thought Sandy was dying or something. I forgot where we were playing bridge. Couldn't find the room. Or Bob. Wandered around like a nut." She flushed, further enhancing her beauty. "Bet I woke up half the guests in the other wing of the motel. How embarrassing!"

"Forget it," her husband advised.

"I'll never forget it." The relief in her voice was genuine. "I'm going to sleep with Sandra tonight. Wouldn't get a wink with her alone in there."

"Most probably it'll never happen again," Brennan said as he started to leave. "But remember the paper sack if it does."

119

"We can't thank you enough, Dr. Brennan." Jennifer Parker offered him a sincere smile and a warm handclasp. "What would we have done without you?"

"Yeah, Doc," her handsome spouse said. "How much do I owe you for all your trouble?"

"Nothing," Brennan answered. "Forget it. Glad to be of help. Now, it's back to bed for me. I've got a big day ahead tomorrow—guess it's today by now."

He shook hands with Mr. Parker, smiled at his stunning wife, gathered his robe about him and walked out into the cold night air.

Once back in his own room he immediately got back into bed and lay shivering under the blankets, feeling exhausted but satisfied.

Jackie looked at the high window of her cell. The heavy steel bars fascinated her. They looked more ominous than usual at night. It would all be so simple. Just stand on the end of the bunk and tie the belt of her bathrobe to the bars, then around her neck. And step off. It would be finished. It would be easy. But she knew she'd never do it. She rolled over to face the wall. She brought her knees up to her chest and lay staring at the rough plaster, seeing nothing.

It was not the cell or being in jail that was tormenting her. Christ, the only relief she got anymore was when she was left alone. It was all the poking and nosing into her private affairs that got to her. Like that new doctor.

He was something else. Big, tall pediatrician. Big quack. With a big nose. Well, she'd showed him. He didn't get anything out of ol' Jackie, that's for damn sure. So let him waste his time too, just like all those other dumb bastards. She could care less.

But, God, it got to her. The constant investigating. Dragging her into this or that courtroom. It was like she was some kind of animal in a zoo. Who wouldn't think of end-ing it all, of stepping into a homemade noose. But Jackie knew she'd never really go that route. She knew suicide was a sin.

Jackie wasn't real sure if she believed in God anymore. But she did know about sin. And she knew she believed in it. The only halfway smart person she'd run into in this whole mess was the jail chaplain, Reverend Maass. He really knew about sin.

The reverend didn't bug her about poor little Helen all the time like everybody else did. When he came around, he'd just read the Bible—always the Old Testament—the interesting parts, like Sodom and Gomorrah. And they'd talk about sin and pray.

Jackie wasn't too sure praying did any good, but the reverend sure was hooked on it. He looked so serious, sitting in that straight chair in the visiting room, left hand on his forehead, elbow on his knee, eyes closed. He always had on the same black suit. She had noticed it was getting a little shiny here and there. But it was clean. Like his white shirt and his polished shoes. Yeah, the reverend knew how to take care of what he had. And he knew how to pray.

"Lord, God, Jesus Christ," he'd begin. Always the same. Like he was talking to three guys, trying to get their attention all at once so he wouldn't have to repeat himself.

"Lord, God, Jesus Christ—we're all sinners." Even with his eyes closed, he always seemed to know if Jackie didn't nod at this point. He'd tense up and stop. Just a little nod from her, and he'd go on.

The rest of his praying was no different. Different words, maybe, but the same meaning. Sin, sin, sin. He didn't hold out much hope for anybody. He acted like he knew everybody was damned. Oh, the reverend would mention the repentance bit now and again, but Jackie could tell he didn't really buy it himself. It was a part of his act, though, so he had to mention it briefly before getting back to the main thing—the sin.

Reverend Maass was only about thirty-five, she guessed. Neat. Clean. Well-groomed hair, all in place. On the thin side.

He never bothered her. He didn't get personal or picky like all the others. And that was a relief. He just wanted to pray. And once he got going, there was no stopping him. Jackie had often thought during her sessions with him, that if she got up real quietly and left, he'd probably never even notice it. He'd probably just go on alone. Talking to the Lord and God and Jesus Christ about sin.

Late at night, like now, was the only time you could hear yourself think around this jailhouse. Only time you had any privacy, too.

During the day it was something else. Buckets and dishes banging around, swearing, yelling, laughing, radios blaring out country music—every kind of noise you could think of came from the men's section down the hall. Jackie had a private cell. She was the only woman in the jail. Occasionally on weekends they'd put some drunken old broad in with her. They'd mostly lay on the extra bunk and snore and slobber all night, then get out the next day.

Couple of times they'd put one of those young runaways in for a day or two. Skinny kids with long straight hair and dirty jeans. One kid, she remembered, hadn't had any shoes, and it was winter. And Jackie could still remember that horrible musky perfume she'd had on. The smell had hung on for days after the kid was picked up or sent home or whatever.

Another, Jackie was sure, had had some kind of V.D. Always going to the pot, and crying when she did. Scared the hell out of Jackie. She made them get her some of that germ spray and really gave the place a cleaning and spraying after that one left. Had to. You can catch some of those things pretty easy. Especially around toilets.

But mostly Jackie was alone in the Ross County Jail. Alone

122

in the women's section, that is. And it was better alone. She didn't have to talk or listen to any stupid questions. She could think. She could sleep whenever she felt like it. She could sit and daydream for hours if she wanted to. Funny—she'd been doing that a lot lately. She'd been having a lot of dreams at night, too. More than usual, anyway.

She'd had one of the dreams before. She guessed she'd had it off and on for as far back as she could remember. In the dream she was a very little girl and she'd been bad. It was all real vague. She didn't really know what she'd done. But she knew it must've been bad because of the way she felt— all shivery and excited and expecting something. Yeah, she'd been bad all right. And in the dream, she enjoyed it. She knew she shouldn't, but she couldn't help herself. It was a delicious, irresistible feeling.

Then it would come to her—always in just this order. She'd realize what she'd done. Suddenly she'd see that the arm was off her Raggedy Ann. The next thing she knew, she'd be holding one button-eye between her teeth and throwing the gray cotton stuffing all around. Pulling and throwing and laughing between her clenched teeth.

Next it got dark. From gray to black, real quick. Sort of like a very cold shadow. She was scared. She was sitting there on the floor in a heap of stuffing and she was shrinking. And it was getting darker. She couldn't get smaller fast enough. Something hit her. She couldn't get away from it. Then there was noise—a lot of noise. Then fear. And pain.

So she swallowed the button-eye and held her breath. That made it all go away. That always stopped it. That was the end of the dream.

Funny thing, she'd had it so long it didn't much bother her. It was sort of familiar, like an old favorite thing. Not frightening. Lots of things were scary to Jackie. Mostly people. But not her favorite dream.

It wasn't that she was really physically afraid of others.

123

It was just that she didn't trust them. She guessed she really didn't trust anybody. It used to bother her a lot, but not anymore. That was another thing she'd had to learn the hard way.

Jackie remembered starting school. It was a frightening thing in itself, but all the other kids seemed scared too. The teacher, Miss Encina, helped them all get over being afraid. It took a while, but pretty soon Jackie liked school.

She liked Miss Encina too. The teacher was little and pretty, dark haired, and soft. Jackie particularly remembered her soft voice.

Jackie would do just about anything to please Miss Encina. She knew her letters and numbers way before the rest of the kids. Her hand was always the first one up. She had to work pretty hard, but it was worth it. Miss Encina would always smile when Jackie gave the right answer to a question.

One day Jackie discovered something else. She had a stomach ache and felt real bad. Miss Encina called her up to her big desk and, in a whisper asked what was wrong.

"My tummy hurts," she remembered replying.

"Do you have to go to the bathroom, honey?" Miss Encina asked.

"No, ma'am."

"Well," she said as she pushed her chair back and held out her arms, "why don't you just sit here on my lap for a little while, and I'll bet your tummy will feel better real fast."

Jackie snuggled into Miss Encina's lap, her arms as far around the pretty lady as she could reach. Miss Encina went on teaching the class, occasionally giving Jackie a smile and a hug of reassurance. Sure enough, in a while Jackie fell asleep in her lap. When she woke up from her nap, her tummy ache was gone. She felt great.

Jackie remembered she got a lot of tummy aches in school after that. And Miss Encina could always make them go away.

But one day when Jackie stood by the big desk, rubbing her eyes with one hand, holding her stomach with the other, Miss Encina just sat there. She stared at Jackie, then finally said, "Well, Jacqueline, if you're sick again, perhaps I'd better phone your mother. Send you on home."

She never calls me Jacqueline, the girl had suddenly realized. Then it hit her. Call mother. Send her away. "I think I'll be all right in a little while," she'd said. Then she walked back to her own desk. As Jackie recalled it, it was a very long walk.

Wonder what had prompted Fearless Jim to creep into town tonight. First time she'd laid eyes on him since he moved out of the house. God, he'd acted shifty. That's what had prompted her to say, "You look like you're the one who has to go to court in a couple of days. That's not a bad idea, come to think of it. Think I'll tell the judge you did it."

"Now, damn it, Jackie," he'd said, "don't you joke 'bout that."

Jackie remembered how he'd kept looking around the room the whole time. Except he never looked directly at her, though, or at Hank Bond, the evening jailer sitting just outside the open door of the visiting room.

"Why did you come now?" she'd asked.

"Well—"

She continued to stare at her nervous husband. At least she guessed he was still her husband. Maybe the bastard already got a divorce. Who gave a damn?

"It's er—sure is good to see you, Jackie. You, ah, you look O.K."

"Oh, I'm just dandy. Do you like my dress?" Jackie's hands traced her figure inside the shapeless grey sack. It's the latest thing, you know. Made in Dwight—in the Women's State Prison. Everybody's wearing it this year."

"Don't be that way," her husband whined. "It ain't right."

125

"What the hell would you know about what's right," she hissed back at him. "What're you bothering me for anyway? Get out of here."

"Now, Jackie—" Jim Teal sat looking wounded and wondering just why he'd bothered to come back to Rossdale. Then he thought of something. "Monica said to tell you hello."

Jackie was about to continue her attack, but his remark stopped her for a moment. She looked down at her hands, then asked softly, "How is she?"

"Oh, she's just fine," Jim replied happily. He was glad to have found a subject he could talk about, a subject that gave him some sort of reason for coming to see his wife. "She goes to a day care center. Likes it a lot. Sort of like a nursery school. Sis works, you know. She and Sis get on just fine. I tell you, I never saw Monica so happy."

"Thanks. That's just what I wanted to hear," Jackie snapped.

"Now Jackie, I didn't mean no harm. I mean—don't want to hurt—"

She coldly and easily stared him down. Could I really have been this hard up, she wondered. What a prize I did marry.

Teal, realizing he'd again used the wrong approach, changed his tone and said loudly, "Now you just listen here, Jackie. You just—"

"Leave me alone," she spat back at him. "Just leave me alone."

"What's the matter here?" demanded the jailer, putting aside his copy of **Playboy.**

"Get him out. Get rid of him," Jackie said shrilly.

"You better leave now," Hank Bond said to Jim Teal. "A prisoner's got rights, you know. If she don't want to see you, she don't have to."

"O.K.," Teal answered. He didn't want to make trouble in this town. "I'll go."

Jim got to his feet, nervously kneading his winter cap with

126

his hands, and stared at his angry wife for another second. Then he turned and dejectedly shuffled toward the door. Once there, he glanced back at his woman. "Ain't there nothin' I can do for you, Jackie?"

The tenor of his voice stayed any further outburst from Jackie. She looked at him and suddenly realized she might never see this mate of hers again. "No, Jim. Just go on back to Chicago."

"Nothin'?"

"Nothing." Jackie wished he'd give it up. Why prolong this? They had no feelings for each other anymore. They were just remembering an old habit, that's all.

"Sure?"

"Ain't he ever going to give up?" she muttered. Perhaps if she gave him some stupid chore, he'd get the hell out of her life. "Well, you might stop at the motel and see a doctor named Brennan. He's been nosing around. Maybe it'd do some good if you talked to him."

"Sure, Jackie," he answered gratefully. "Doc Brennan. Sure, I'll go look him up right now. Bye, Jackie."

Happy little moron, she thought as she remembered her husband's belated visit. Well, at least she'd gotten rid of him. He and Brennan would make a good pair. She chuckled to herself and decided they definitely deserved each other.

She couldn't get to sleep. It had to be very late by now. Of course most days she did nothing, just layed around in her cell, so she had no reason to be tired. Actually, today— must be yesterday by now—had been the busiest day she'd had for several weeks.

Monica was happy, Jim had said. Jackie guessed she was glad to hear it. But it bothered her somehow. Damn it, Monica belonged to her, not to that pissy-assed sister of her husband's. Old no-balls James was still trying to ignore his responsibilities, farming out his first-born to that fat, smelly sister of his. Poor Monica.

127

Her lawyer, Mr. Delaney, had made it all extremely clear to her, and she didn't like it. It was all wrong—very wrong. But she couldn't change it and neither could he. Either she pleaded guilty or she'd end up in the electric chair. She gave up or they'd fry her ass.

Hell, she'd known that all along. It bothered Mr. Delaney a lot more than it did her. Took a long time for him to come around to accepting what she'd known from the day Helen died. Just goes to show, book learning doesn't make you smart. You got to have common sense. Like Jackie did.

That damn carrot-headed lawyer of hers was actually disappointed when the psychiatrists found her sane. Stupid shyster actually wanted her declared nuts. Probably would've made his job a lot easier or something.

Boy, that's the one thing ol' Jackie would never hold still for. No way! Those three doctors the court ordered to check her out gave her some really bad times, but she finally convinced them. Next person who even hinted she was crazy was going to get a fat lip.

Lord, she missed her kids. Both of them. But nothing could help Helen now. And Monica couldn't live in a jail cell.

Sometimes Jackie thought she'd go nuts just out of sheer loneliness. Those kids were hers. She had a right to at least have Monica. Especially now. She needed the consolation her daughter could give her.

It was all so silly, really. So ridiculous. No one could understand. Not in a million years. They said she'd killed Helen. Hell, she loved that baby. Loved her too much. If she was the kind of monster everybody thought she was, Helen would've been cut up in little pieces long before now.

Christ, nobody cared. Nobody believed Jackie. Not about Helen. Not about anything in her whole damn life.

It was all so simple. So simple it was unbelievable. Jackie had wanted just one thing for her daughters. She wanted a better life for the girls than she'd had. And she knew that wouldn't happen by accident. There was nothing to all that old crap about luck, or good fortune, or fate being kind.

She knew that. She'd been the route. What had luck ever done for her? Did fate give her Jim Teal as a way to get away from her parents? Big deal. Christ, the Rossdale jail was better than living at home with her folks any day. So if Jim Teal was the best fate could come up with, then to hell with it.

It sounded like Monica was doing just fine. Just proved Jackie'd done a good job of raising her. Given a little more time, she'd have had Helen shaped up too. Helen was just beginning to get the idea. Course she was harder to train than Monica, but Jackie knew she shouldn't compare her children. She knew she couldn't expect one to get along as fast as the other.

Yeah, Helen would probably have turned out to be a real good girl. Like her sister. She would've made the grade.

Why did she have to be so goddamn stubborn? Probably got it from her daddy's side of the family. Helen knew her mother loved her. Why, all Jackie had to do was hold out her arms and she'd run right to her. And she just loved to be held real close and kissed and sweet-talked. Helen would purr like a kitten when she and Jackie were all snuggled up.

And they said she abused Helen. They said she killed her baby. They were crazy. She loved her little doll, and Helen loved her. But people couldn't understand real love. Probably because they never had anybody care enough to try to help them. So no use trying to convince them. They were hopeless. Sad, but hopeless.

But they were the ones with power. Big deal. Who wanted it? Who needed it? Just the kind of sick nut who put her in jail. They had to have power, because they didn't have anything else. They didn't have a mother who'd take the time to teach them right from wrong or how to get along in the world. No they had none of the important training.

And since they couldn't get along with each other, they had to find something to take the place of proper raising. And they found out about power and made it their god. You either loved power or you were wrong.

Jackie knew this society was built on sand. She knew it was unstable. She knew it because she'd gone through a lot of hell just to be able to understand it.

And by God, she owed her girls the benefit of her experience. So she taught them. And they learned.

Sure, Monica got it a lot quicker than Helen, but she was the oldest. The oldest always gets all the breaks. But even stubborn little Helen was coming along pretty well. If Jackie could've had just a little more time with her, Helen would've been just fine.

CHAPTER XI

Harold Keller waited for his secretary to get the telephone call through to the psychiatrist. Getting one of those birds on the phone was usually an all-day job he'd learned. Consequently, he'd placed the call quite early this morning. Finally she announced that Dr. Greenglass was on the wire.

"Hello, Doctor, this is Mr. Keller, state's attorney of Ross County," he began.

"Yes, Mr. Keller. What is your decision?" the psychiatrist asked indifferently.

"I'll definitely need you in court tomorrow, Doctor. Have to have you here in Rossdale," Keller answered. "Very important to the resolution of the Teal case. Very important."

"Mr. Keller," Greenglass continued coldly, "I've been a witness in just about every kind of crime imaginable. And in most of the courts in northern Illinois. Not to mention a fair number of out-of-state cases. I believe it's customary to give the witness a bit more notice than just a single day."

"You're right, Doctor. Absolutely right," Keller agreed apologetically. "But something has come up at this eleventh hour. Something only you can refute. No, that's not it. Only a doctor of your vast experience can possibly keep the case in a reasonable perspective. I must insist that you attend in the morning."

"Oh, all right, Keller," Dr. Greenglass said irritably. "I'll see you at nine in the morning. And you can expect my expense

131

voucher to reflect the fact that I'll have to cancel out all my appointments for tomorrow. Goodbye, Mr. Keller."

The state's attorney returned the telephone to its cradle and smiled smugly. He had little or no interest in the amount of the psychiatrist's bill. He knew the county would only pay what he authorized as a fair witness fee, regardless of the doctor's charges. Of course, in future cases he might have to switch mental experts, but that really presented no problem.

He felt that brilliant little effort should neutralize any effect the testimony of Dr. Patrick Brennan might possibly have on the outcome of tomorrow's hearing. Fight fire with fire, he thought.

He would certainly win a life sentence for the Teal woman. And that should go a long way toward assuring the re-election of State's Attorney Keller. All he'd have to do was wait until some circuit judge died, then he could move into that very appealing vacancy.

Died, he thought, or was so discredited in the eyes of the community that he'd elect to retire. With the judicial reforms of the early 60's, judges ran on their record in office. The separate ballot asked, "Should Judge Waggoner be retained? Yes or no." No party label. This made it virtually impossible for a judge to be thrown out of office. Unless, of course, he fouled up so terribly that he provoked a rebellion among the voters. Unlikely, Harold reminded himself. Still, this Teal case was rather uniformly abhorrent to the public. If Waggoner tried to get tricky, who could predict what reaction might ensue?

In the meantime, Keller reminded himself, he must be fully prepared for Friday's hearing. Leave no openings that Mr. Delaney or Dr. Brennan or Judge Waggoner or anybody else could possibly exploit at the expense of his own career. He'd send Jacqueline Teal to prison with a life sentence. Then he should be comfortably secure.

His strategy session was interrupted by the squawking intercom. "Yes, yes," Harold muttered impatiently.

"A Mr. and Mrs. Parker and daughter to see you," his receptionist announced.

"Who? Parker. Don't know them. What about? What do they want?"

She sighed, as was her habit when dealing with her irascible boss. Miss Jensen's father was a very powerful precinct committeeman in the local Republican Party. He also served on the central committee and exerted considerable control over just who in the local party structure would be supported for what political office. So she had long ago stopped trying to be civil to Harold Keller. She considered him totally impossible and generally ignored him. With the lack of patience she would normally reserve for an impudent teenager, she continued, "They want to see you about Dr. Brennan. I'll send them on back."

The intercom clicked off before Keller could voice a complaint. He leaped up, intending to berate Miss Jensen in person, but before he could get around his desk, a strikingly handsome couple and a pretty blond child appeared in the doorway. "Come in," Keller stuttered, his face still red with anger.

"Thank you," a stern-faced Robert Parker responded. "Sorry to take up your valuable time." he continued. "Good of you to see us. Perhaps my daughter Sandra could wait with your secretary—at least for now."

Who had a choice, Harold wondered. Aloud. he asked his unsolicited visitors, "What's this about Dr. Brennan. Mr. Parker? What can I do for you? Help—?"

"I need that very much. Mr. Keller." Robert Parker interrupted. "Help, that is. I can only pray I get it here."

Keller's interest in his guest mounted when he noticed Mrs. Parker blotting at her eyes with a crumpled tissue. "I don't understand, Mr. Parker," he said. "What's this all about?"

"Child molesting, Mr. Keller. The digusting pawing of my little girl by that medical charlatan, Brennan."

"Molesting?" Harold squeaked. "Dr. Brennan? A child?"

"My child!" Parker shouted. His wife sobbed aloud.

"This some joke, Mr. Parker?" Harold asked in abject disbelief. "It has to be. That's it, all some sort of silly jest. Well, I have no time for this sort of thing. No time at all."

"You'll have time for me, Mr. Keller," Parker said with cold conviction. "I came through that damn snowstorm just to see you." He pointed to the window. Huge white flakes were falling so rapidly they almost totally obscured the view. "I called the police, and some impudent cop told me to come here and sign a complaint. I'm here and I'm not leaving until I'm sure that bastard Brennan is going to get what he deserves."

Ah, the luxury of it all, Brennan thought as he lingered over a second cup of coffee in the motel dining room. He'd slept until after nine o'clock—a very rare indulgence indeed for a busy pediatrician. A refreshing shower, a leisurely break-fast—who cared if there was a blizzard outside. All was right with his world at the moment.

He realized that this cherished respite would be short-lived. Soon he'd have to go back to work on the Teal case. There were a few odds and ends to clear up, but he mostly needed to mentally organize all he'd learned during the past few days. Tomorrow was court day.

Reluctantly, Brennan signed his check and walked out into the lobby. He was surprised, though not pleasantly, to see Captain Miller stomping up and down in the entryway, shaking the snow off his shoes and coat. "Looking for me?" Brennan asked as Miller came into the lobby.

"Yes. Let's go to your room."

Always the curt bastard, Brennan thought. He led the way. Both men had to go through the stomping routine at his door. In and settled, Brennan asked, "What now, Captain Miller?"

"Now we discuss the Brennan case," Miller answered as he extracted a small loose-leaf notebook from his coat pocket. "Funny, the Brennan case requires my attention now. Not the Teal case. It makes everything a little more personal."

"Care to tell me what you mean Captain? Or am I supposed to guess? Don't tell me—I know. You figured I'd be snowed in today, so you came over to keep me company. How nice." Brennan dropped the sarcasm from his voice and continued, "Well, what the hell do you want, Miller? I have important things to do today."

"So have I, Doctor, and you're it."

"Oh Christ." Brennan did not try to conceal his exasperation.

Miller, ignoring his host's anger, confided, "Got a hurry-up call to go to the state's attorney's office about an hour ago. You know a Parker family, Doc?"

"Yes," Brennan answered in a more reasonable tone. "I know them."

"The Parkers just signed a complaint against you."

"They signed a what?"

"A criminal complaint. They say you sexually molested their daughter, Sandra, last night."

"Molested? Sandra? You've got to be kidding, Miller. Why I never—"

"You deny the allegation then, Dr. Brennan."

"Of course I deny it. Molested their kid—oh my God."

"I have to investigate this," Miller said in a matter-of-fact tone. "That's why I'm here."

Brennan was silent for a moment, then disbelievingly asked, "You can't be serious, Miller! Not for a moment. You don't think I molested any child?"

"Doc," the policeman calmly replied, "you remember that lecture you gave me for free on Tuesday. The one about me making a preformed judgment in an investigation and then manufacturing evidence to fit it. Remember?"

"Of course."

"Well, you're about to learn firsthand that's not the way I operate," Miller said. "And understand right now that this is not my doing. The Parkers went to the state's attorney. They said you molested their Sandra. They charged you with a felony—one, I might add, that is usually taken very seriously here in Rossdale. Last guy convicted of indecent liberties with a minor drew five to fifteen years in Joliet for it. That's about the average sentence, I'd say.

"So, you're accused, and I've heard their side of the story. They're down at the courthouse right now giving their sworn depositions about the monster who defiled their daughter. That's you, Doc.

"Now I'm here to investigate the case—your case. And I haven't prejudged anything. You understand that? Nothing. I'm asking you for your side of the story."

"Yes," Brennan whispered as he slumped further into his chair. He felt as if he were suddenly a thousand years old. None of this made any sense. He sat and stared at the policeman.

"O.K. We've got to do this right." Miller went to the doorway, opened it, and waved to someone in the hall. Within seconds a uniformed police sergeant joined them. "My witness," Miller said simply, without bothering to make any further introductions.

"Now, Brennan, this is the deal. You can talk or remain silent. You have the right to have an attorney. If you can't afford a lawyer, one will be provided by the county. And," the captain added ominously, "anything you say may be used against you. Understand all this?"

Brennan nodded.

"All right, then, let's get down to business. First, you can read and sign this paper. It's all about your rights which we just went over." Miller waited for Brennan to sign, then continued, "What're we going to do, Brennan? Do we talk about the charges or do you yell for a lawyer? I'll tell you, for what it's worth, that any attorney would advise you not to say a word to me. They're very consistent and insistent about that. You're supposed to shut up and say nothing, even if the charge is spitting on the sidewalk."

Brennan stood up and walked to the window. He lit a cigarette and was silent for quite a long time. "Sure is snowing out there," he said at last. He turned to face his accuser. "Can you tell me something of the details of this crime, Captain?"

"I guess so," Grant Miller responded. "You met the Parkers in the dining room last night. Just a casual conversation, they say. About eleven, Mrs. Parker left a bridge game to check on Sandra. Sure enough, she was having one of her nervous spells. Mrs. Parker says she has them occassionally, especially in any circumstance different from her usual routine. She remembered the nice doctor from dinner, thought he might be able to give Sandra a sedative. That usually brings her out of the fit or whatever it is—something about her breathing that sets it off. I didn't understand that too clearly.

"Anyway, she knocks on your door—she'd seen you going in or out of your room earlier—and asks you for help. Sure, glad to, you say.

"Mrs. Parker reports you got very excited about her daughter's condition. This sort of alarmed her. Their doctor at home in Indianapolis always took Sandra's spells as a rather routine thing. A shot, a snooze, and that was the end of it.

"So the mother goes off to fetch her husband—"

"Then what did I do?" Brennan interrupted. "Rape Sandy?"

Miller ignored the physician's taunting. "Sandra picks up the story here. She swears you told her she had to be examined in case there was something radically wrong with her. She

137

describes—all this was very embarrassing to the child, you understand—how you—"

"Captain, this is a bunch of shit," Brennan pronounced angrily. "I hope to hell you realize it."

"Don't you want to hear what you did to the kid, Doc?" Miller asked. Brennan signaled for Miller to continue.

"Sandra Parker related how you fondled her budding breasts, ran your hands all over her, then put your fingers in her—'down there' were her exact words for it."

"The little liar," Brennan snorted. "She said that?"

"Sure did, Doc. Now let me finish. At this point the parents returned and were pleased to see that Sandra was O.K. You'd cured her without any shot or sedative or anything. They were really impressed.

"Anyway, you hurried them out of Sandra's room and into theirs. You then gave them a very long lecture about Sandra's condition. They now realize the real reason for your apparent concern—you were stalling for time."

"Jesus Christ, Miller! This is ridiculous. Absolutely ridiculous!"

"You asked to hear it, Doc. Now, what's your story?"

"Captain, if all this happened around midnight, why the hell did these concerned parents sleep on it all night? Why wait till morning?"

"Forgot, Doc. Parker explained how Sandra was naturally terrified by this experience and ashamed—as if being passive while you molested her was some kind of sin in itself. She was afraid to say anything about it, in spite of the fact that her mother stayed in her room last night.

"This morning her parents, especially her mom, sensed something was still wrong with their daughter. Mrs. Parker, after much questioning, finally got the story out of Sandra."

Brennan left the window, walked away from the whiteness of the snow accumulating outside. He collapsed into a chair, flung one leg over the armrest, and rounded his shoulders.

In a low voice he began relating the events of the evening before. "I talked with Jim Teal in the bar. He was here last night. Saw his wife. Afterwards, he drove out to talk to me. I was glad to get the chance to see him."

He looked at Miller. The policeman's face was an expressionless mask. He continued, "I went to my room. Was reading in bed. Must have been about eleven when this Mrs. Parker came banging on my door." Brennan continued his version of the events of the night before. Miller did not interrupt him. At last he concluded his long monologue with, "That's it. And it's the truth."

"What about this tetany thing?" Miller asked. "That on the level?"

"I thought so at the time," Brennan answered. "Believed it was involuntary. Hysteria. But anyone can put himself into it by breathing as fast as he can. In light of this molesting charge, I'm sure it was all faked."

"Did you ever know or see the Parkers before yesterday?"

"Never."

The captain stared at Brennan for a long time. Finally, he seemed to have reached a decision. "O.K., Doc, that's your story. I got work to do."

He rose, put on his coat and hat, then turned to face Brennan again. "You're to stay in Rossdale, Doc. You're not off the hook by a long shot. I have a lot of investigating to do. When I'm done there'll be an arrest. I'm putting you on a leash for now, a short one, so don't try to run away. That would be a sure admission of guilt. Besides, you couldn't get very far in all this snow."

CHAPTER XII

The snow was still falling. Brennan observed the rather futile efforts of a motel employee who periodically passed his window. The man would shovel all the snow off the walkway, then immediately go back and repeat the whole process.

That guy and I have a lot in common, Brennan thought. He gets nowhere for all his endeavor, and I sit here pondering the mess I'm in without accomplishing anything.

But what could he do? The molesting charge was really out of his hands. Now it was up to the police, the lawyers, and the courts. Brennan experienced deep fear and anguish as he saw his original purpose for being in Rossdale fade away.

He wondered what he was supposed to do about the Teal case. Would the judge still want to use him as a witness? It was unlikely. He realized he should call somebody or do something to get out of that damn mess. After all, now he had a mess all his own.

Brennan speculated as to whether Waggoner would hear his child molesting case. God, what a thought. The judge brings an expert to Rossdale, only to have him end up as an accused felon in his own court.

Brennan knew he was avoiding the main issue by worrying about the Teal case and watching the snow pile up outside. What he had to do was look directly at the abhorrent molesting charge. The thought made him shudder with anxiety and frustration. He had heard or read about this sort of thing happening to other physicians, but he had never seriously worried about it. Nevertheless, he'd violated the rule—never, under any circumstances, examine or treat a female patient without a witness present.

Of course here he'd had little choice. The mother had rushed out of the motel room before he could stop her. And that damn brat, who'd certainly seemed to be in need of treatment at the time, had conjured up all this sex stuff about him.

Wait a minute, Brennan thought. The parents lied too. Last night they knew nothing about hysterical tetany. This morning it was just another of Sandy's frequent spells. Look at it, Brennan commanded himself. The parents lied. The kid lied. You've been had.

But why? Why would these strangers do this to him? What could they possibly hope to gain by destroying Dr. Patrick Brennan? Think about it. Any number of people in Rossdale would be delighted to see him ruined. Perhaps some citizens' committee, outraged over his meddling in the Teal case, was behind it all. Or perhaps the Parkers were really outraged local citizens themselves. If so, was Captain Miller in on the conspiracy? Or maybe it was all just a sick coincidence. Maybe the Parkers were professional extortionists who had arbitrarily chosen him as their victim.

Whatever their reasons, the Parkers had done a good job. Any credibility he had in regard to the Teal trial was now down the drain. And the effects of this mess would certainly not be limited to Rossdale. As soon as the word got out, the St. Louis newspapers would pick it up, his patients' parents would learn of it, and that would do it. He could just imagine what the mothers' reactions would be when they found out that their pediatrician had been charged with child molesting.

No doubt his life would be considerably modified by the recent events in Rossdale. Even if he fought and won, his reputation would still be tarnished, if not totally wrecked.

His new book would now have not even a remote chance of becoming a success. And the pediatric practice he'd spent a lifetime building would crumble in a matter of weeks. Merely the hint of his being a dirty old man was totally devastating to everything he'd ever had or wanted.

It was all too ironic. Every action, every event of the past few months seemed to have contributed to Brennan's basic discontent with his way of life. There had been far too many unsatisfying experiences of late. Parents, always a thorny problem in pediatrics, seemed to have attained new heights of stupidity and demand and plan old noxious carping recently. There had been few, if any, offsetting cases of real medical interest. He felt he'd become the snotty-nosed-kid specialist. In the past his work had soothed and sustained him, and his life had been rich in reward. This was no longer true.

Take this Parker thing. He'd responded to a call for help. And he'd been able to help—to cure the kid. He'd shown the Parkers kindness and sympathy as well, and they had responded to all this by accusing him of sexual indecency.

By God, Brennan resolved, to hell with the healing arts. He was sick of being a damn Asclepian slave. Let some other nut treat the brats. It was time for him to live a little. Parick Brennan was through with the practice of medicine.

Suddenly there was a pounding on his door. Christ what now? Probably the police. He immediately experienced a myriad of unpleasant bodily sensations that he recognized as an involuntary animal reaction to stark fear.

The rapping grew more insistent. Brennan extended a hesitant hand and opened the door. On the threshold stood a very agitated gentleman who looked as if he were wearing pajamas under his coat. Then Patrick recognized the local coroner, Dr. Winston. And he was wearing a surgical scrub suit beneath his overcoat. "I need you, Dr. Brennan. Need your help—now. Let's go."

143

Relief flooded through Brennan, leaving him weak yet considerably comforted. "Come on in, Doctor. Tell me about it." He extended a still-sweaty hand toward his visitor.

"No. You come. Grab your coat. You see—ah hell, I'll tell you in the car. Come along, man!"

Brennan followed the younger physician out to the car that he had left idling in front of the main entrance. Once they were underway, skidding and sliding through the blizzard, Brennan asked, "Now what's this all about?"

"I got trouble, and you're my only hope. While ago I delivered a gravida five mother. She's RH-negative. Had one baby that lived. Lost the next three—probably all died of the hemolytic disease. At any rate, with this fifth pregnancy, she's had a hell of a high anti-Rh titer, indicating severe fetal stress. But the kid didn't die in utero. She was scheduled to go on up to Rockford for this delivery. The pediatricians there were to be all set up for an exchange transfusion. She wasn't due for another month, but they were going to induce her labor in a couple of weeks. All arranged. Then late this morning she went into premature labor. Couldn't go anywhere with all this damn snow—even if there was time, which there wasn't.

"The delivery was O.K. The baby weighed a little over five and a half pounds. But that kid's sick as hell, Brennan. Little boy. He's had it if he doesn't get an exchange transfusion—right now. And nobody around here knows their butt from a barrel about this damn disease or how to treat it. I was ready to give up—make a few futile gestures to satisfy the parents and watch the little guy die. Then I remembered you were still in town. So you gotta do it. You gotta take care of this baby. You're the only one. And he's a very precious infant."

"They all are, Karl." Brennan looked out at the snow swirling around the car. Now why would he say a thing like

144

that? Hadn't he just resolved to divorce himself from all this sort of humbug?

He was silent for an overlong moment, then he shrugged and asked, "Have you got any laboratory results on the little one yet?"

"Yeah. Coombs test is strongly positive. Baby's very pale, anemic as hell. And he's getting worse. The blood from the umbilical cord had eleven grams of hemoglobin. Checked it about forty-five minutes later and the hemoglobin was down to eight grams."

"What blood type is the mother? How high was her anti-Rh titer? You order any blood for the transfussion yet?"

"Mom is O-negative. Baby is O-positive. Her titer got up to 1 to 256 a couple of weeks ago. Lord knows what it is right now. I ordered a unit of fresh blood, type O-negative, crossmatched with the baby and the mother. Just like the book says. I had to look all this jazz up. That okay?"

"Perfect. When will the blood be ready to transfuse?"

"Should be ready as soon as we can get to the hospital and get it going."

"I hope so, Karl." Brennan, frowning pensively, lit a cigarette. "Sounds like this kid is hovering on the brink of heart failure. You know, the way that hemoglobin is dropping, this is going to be very risky. Parents know the score?"

"Yes. Hell, they lost the last three. They know!"

"Well, there's a chance here. A very slim chance, but we have to try."

Brennan was as familiar with the intricacies of this Rh disease as he was with the back of his right hand. In some instances where the mother was Rh-negative, meaning her blood lacked the Rh factor, and the baby was Rh-positive, meaning his blood did contain the Rh factor, microscopic amounts of the baby's red blood cells would leak into the mother's bloodstream. To her system these cells represented a foreign substance. Her internal defense mechanisms auto-

145

matically manufactured antibodies that coated the alien Rh-positive cells and caused their destruction.

This was all well and good as far as the mother was concerned. The trouble was that during pregnancy this maternal antibody, which was not a cell but a humoral protein, could pass through the placenta into the fetal circulation, where it destroyed the baby's Rh-positive blood cells. If the rate of destruction exceeded the rate of production of new blood cells, the baby became anemic. If the anemia became profound, the infant's heart would begin to fail. And this was one highly fatal situation. Death often resulted either before or shortly after birth.

The only chance in a case as severe as the one Dr. Winston had described was to get the antibody-saturated blood out of the baby and replace it with Rh-negative blood, which would be immune to the destructive capacity of any antibodies that remained in the infant's system.

Karl Winston wheeled his car into a Doctors Only parking slot, and they hurried into the two-story, brick hospital. Minutes later they were in the dressing room of the small surgical suite. Brennan threw off his street clothing and donned a scrub suit. Dr. Winston picked up the phone, dialed the laboratory, and asked about the progress of the blood needed for the transfusion.

"The blood donor checked out okay," Winston announced as he hung up the phone. "We can go ahead. I sent for the patient. Anything else?"

"No—Yes. How about an instrument setup? Catheters?"

"The surgical supervisor had to rob some of the standard operative packs, but I think we'll have everything you need. Told them to line up all the sterile plastic catheters. You can take your pick."

"Anesthetist?"

"Waiting. You gonna put the kid under?"

"No, but I want someone to monitor his heart and respiration every second. Damn easy to get cardiac arrest when you change their total blood volume two or three times. But we have to do it to get enough of that lethal factor out of the baby's circulation."

"Okay. Let's scrub." The physicians donned caps and masks and began vigorously washing their hands and arms. In the adjacent operating room, the nurses and the anesthetist prepared the instruments and the very small patient for surgery.

"It's lucky I found you, Brennan. I thought they had you in jail, but when I called—"

"I see you've heard about my alleged transgressions," Brennan interrupted.

Winston peered over his gauze face mask. "Yes. The cops roused me out early this morning to examine the girl and give her a sedative. Sorry. Shouldn't have brought it up."

"Forget it. Let's go to work." Without further conversation, the doctors donned their sterile surgical gowns in the aseptic and ritualistic manner of the operating theater. Hands were gloved with the help of the surgical nurse. Having completed all the preliminaries, both men walked into the operating room to get down to the vital business of the exchange transfusion.

"What's the heart rate doing, Miss?"

"Fast, Dr. Brennan. One-sixty to one-seventy," replied the anesthetist.

Brennan nodded. "Now, I'm going to inject some calcium gluconate into the vein. You know the anticoagulant used to keep it from clotting in the bottle ties it all up, so the blood we're giving the baby is calcium depleted. As we give him this blood, his own blood-calcium level becomes diluted, and he gets irritable and restless. The cardiac rate speeds up, too. Now, this can be tricky. The baby should settle down, and hopefully the pulse will slow and strengthen. Here it goes. Slowly, slowly. Okay?"

"Yes, Doctor."

"Okay. Back to the exchange. Twenty cc's out. Twenty cc's in." A nurse kept a written record of the procedure, recording the volumes of blood removed and replenished. The donor blood was connected to a complicated system of plastic tubes, all controlled by the syringe and stopcocks in Brennan's hands. One catheter extended from the hub to the baby and was threaded deeply into his umbilical vein. Brennan rhythmically withdrew blood in rather small quantities to avoid any further insult to the infant's already stressed cardiovascular system. A flip of levers and this blood, poisonous to the baby, was shot out through another tube and discarded. More flips and the circuitry was readjusted to deliver the same measured amount of donor blood to the calibrated syringe. One final adjustment allowed the "good" blood to flow through the umbilical catheter into the baby. The process continued, and with each exchange, the infant's chances of survival measurably increased.

"Dr. Brennan," called the nurse monitoring the baby's vital signs. Brennan was immediately alerted by the tension in her voice. "Bradycardia. Heartbeat is going down fast. Seventy. Sixty."

"Clamp that oxygen on. Get ready with an endotracheal tube. I may have to open his chest and massage his heart. First, I'll check his venous pressure at this end." After a long moment of silence, Brennan announced, "It's going up. His heart is failing. Maybe he's overloaded. I'll take out some more blood. Reduce the pressure. Reduce the work load of the heart. Keep me posted on that pulse rate."

Brennan withdrew blood. Twenty cc's. Thirty cc's. Should he go for forty? Damn small baby. Damned if you do, damned if you don't, at a time like this.

"Heart rate sixty."

"Heart rate fifty."

"Fifty."

"Get that endotube ready," Brennan commanded. "How's the breathing? Hand me that scalpel. Either this gets better fast or I'll have to open his chest and manually pump his heart. Afraid to take out any more blood. Might shock him. That's all he'd need."

"Breathing not too bad still. Color pink. Heart rate fifty. Fifty. Fifty."

Perspiration dotted the inclined foreheads like a crystalline pox. Any further deterioration in the condition of the infant would necessitate heroic, though usually unsuccessful, resuscitative measures that would greatly compound the problems of this already very sick little boy.

"Fifty. Fifty. Holding at fifty. Hey—sixty. Sixty. Beats up to seventy. Heart sounds are stronger. Heart rate eighty. Ninety. One-ten. One-twenty. One-twenty. Beautiful sounds at one-twenty. Regular." The anesthetist continued her intent scrutiny of the vital signs, then proclaimed, "Stable now, Doctor." A collective sigh of relief echoed off the tiled walls of the operating room.

Patrick Brennan and Karl Winston exhaled, loudly and simultaneously. Neither had realized that he was holding his breath. Both ignored the wave of post-tension lethargy that weakened them. They automatically resumed the interrupted routine of the exchange transfusion.

From under the small rubber oxygen mask a faint, yet insistent whimpering began. The sound gradually became louder and dominated the room. Under their masks, the doctors and nurses smiled. Not only the littlest heart in the place was surging. The older ones were too—with joy and relief and hope.

"Did you ever hear such beautiful crying in all your born days!" Karl Winston said softly.

The doctors entered the mother's room. Dr. Winston made the introductions. "Mary, this is Dr. Brennan. This is Mary Scott."

"Glad to meet you, Dr. Brennan. It—? How is—?"

"Mrs. Scott," Brennan began, "we have just left the nursery. There's a little guy down there in an isolation incubator who said that if we were going by your room to be sure and say hello. And to ask you to stop down and see him when you get a chance."

"He's—? It's—? Oh, thank God, thank God. Is he O.K.? Is he really—all O.K.?"

"He's fine." Patrick Brennan knew that this simple phrase, these few words more than compensated for years of desire, months of discomfort, a few hours of pain, and what must have seemed to the mother like centuries of anticipatory distress.

He watched her reaction. He had been privileged to observe it many times before. She snuggled into the crisp white sheets. Her eyes were sparkling with that very special luminosity that is a mother's. She looked at Dr. Brennan and smiled. It was just a little smile. But it was the Mona Lisa, the Madonna, radiant with the majesty of maternal magic.

"Thank you for giving my son back to me," Mrs. Scott said in a very soft voice.

The tall, lean physician reciprocated the intimate squeeze of her hand. "Mrs. Scott—you, your son, and your doctor—you have all done something very special for me. You may not know it, but that's not important. You have given back to me that which I was accidentally endowed with—the ability to help your son. I kind of lost sight of—oh, never mind. But what I want to say is thank you. Thank you all."

Brennan turned and quietly left the room. Both Mary Scott and Dr. Winston sensed that just now he desired a well-earned moment of seclusion. His unspoken wish was silently acknowledged and honored.

150

CHAPTER XIII

It was late. It was dark. But the darkness was somewhat attenuated by the heavy snow that made the world appear cleaner, softer, quieter, a more attractive place to live. And Patrick Brennan had resolved to continue through life in the only role possible for him—as a doctor. He further swore he would fight this damn molesting charge. Hell, he was no angel, but he damn sure was no child molester. It had to be a frame job that someone had pulled on him. But why in hell—?

Could this be Miller's way of discrediting him? No, Brennan couldn't buy that. He had no love for the cop and he was sure that his feelings were reciprocated. But, he thought, if he was any judge of human nature, Miller was not the sort of guy who'd try to frame someone he disagreed with.

Brennan hurried along the last few steps to his motel room. He unlocked the door, entered, and was not at all pleased to see Grant Miller sprawled across the overstuffed chair. Miller was asleep and snoring loudly. When Brennan shucked off his coat, the snoring ceased. "Sorry. I'm beat," the policeman muttered, trying to suppress a yawn.

"Lot of damn good it does to issue keys around this place."

"Settle down, Doc. This is my town, remember. It's no big thing for me to get a pass key."

"You here to arrest me, Miller? Damn it, I didn't do it. I have no idea what this is all about, but I mean to find out. I'm innocent. I've been framed."

151

"By God, Doc, that's an original story if I've ever heard one!"

"It's the truth! That's the way it had to have happened. Hell, what do you care? All right, throw my ass in jail. I'll get bonded out, or bailed out, or whatever you call it. And I'll prove I'm right. So go ahead, Captain, arrest me!"

"Settle down, Brennan," Miller said. "Bad for your blood pressure to get all worked up. Nobody's here to arrest you."

"What?"

"I said I'm not here to arrest you. Christ, if I'd thought you needed to be arrested, you'd have been in the jug all day."

"That's a relief," Brennan said, relaxing visibly. "Then why are you here?"

"Thought you might be interested to know I solved your case."

"Really, how?" In his enthusiasm Brennan's voice squeaked like a teenager's.

"Did what I'm paid to do. Investigated it," Miller said matter of factly.

"Now, Grant, you have to fill me in on the details of this farce." Brennan's tone and his use of Miller's first name clearly conveyed his desire to make amends with his former adversary.

"That's why I'm here, Doc. But let's go to the bar," Miller said as he stood up. "I have a lot to tell you, but I haven't had a chance to eat all day. A beer and a sandwich would work wonders."

After they had placed their orders, Miller continued. "When I left you earlier, all I had was the Parker's accusation and your denial. No uninvolved witnesses. Your word against theirs. That's about par for this sort of case. So it all boils down to who of those involved is telling the truth."

"I knew your background pretty well. The Parkers were the unknown, so I checked them. Hit pay dirt on the first try. Their address in Indianapolis was a fake. Even their car, complete with Indiana plates, proved to be an Avis rental they picked up in Gary, just over the state line.

"Then I ran a name check on them. Put it out on LEADS."

"What's that?"

"It's our teletype hook-in to the computer. Let's see, the letters mean Law Enforcement Agencies Data Service. They had nothing on the Parkers. Sent the request on to NCIC—that's the National Crime Information Center. Again a blank. No felony record. No idea where they came from or why."

"But you said you solved my case," Brennan interrupted.

"Patience, Doc," Miller said calmly. He held up his empty beer bottle, attracted the eye of their waitress, and held up two fingers. "I put it together this way. It was the Parkers' word against yours. They didn't check out. Therefore, they'd probably come to Rossdale to do the job to you. But thinking is one thing, proving all this is another."

"Why me?" Brennan asked. "If it were a local plot, I could understand. I'm not loved here in your fair city, as you well know."

"Why you? That I don't know, Doc."

"Sorry to interrupt again, Grant. Go on."

"I reasoned the family came to Chicago, picked up the car in Indiana as part of their cover. They probably came to Chicago by plane. So I had to get a little extra-legal at this point in the investigation.

"I asked the maid here to take some extra towels into the Parker kid's room, and if there was a baggage tag on her luggage, to filch it for me." Miller took another drink of beer, extracted a small green and beige tag from his pocket, and handed it to the doctor.

Brennan read it. Delta Air Lines, O'Hare Airport, Chicago, Illinois. Flight 978.

"That's a non-stop flight from Houston, Texas," Miller explained. "Arrives at O'Hare at 10:13 A.M. Just about the right time element if they then went to Gary, rented the car, and

153

drove to Rossdale. They checked in here late yesterday afternoon. It all fits."

"So the Parkers are from Houston." Brennan was impressed with this cop's drive. "Learn anything else about them?"

"Yes." Miller paused to get his cigar going. "I called a captain of detectives I know at the Houston P.D., Captain Murry. He and I were in the same class at the FBI Academy. I mentioned the Parkers. He asked me to describe them and said he would call me back.

"Ten minutes later I got this collect call from Murry. He was calling from a pay booth across the street from police headquarters."

"Sounds mysterious," Brennan observed.

"My thoughts exactly. Anyway, Captain Murry had quite a tale for me. He knew the Parkers, all right. They'd been busted by his vice boys about a year ago. Seems this lovely little family had a thriving business. They made pornographic movies. Real stag stuff. In living color, yet. The three of them—including innocent little Sandra—were the stars in these flicks."

"That little girl, that child!" Brennan was shocked. "You mean to say they used their own kid?"

"Right. Murry said she played the Lolita role. He also said these films had every kind of sexual activity known to man, plus some innovations the Parkers developed themselves."

"My God," Brennan muttered. "If all this was a year ago, why's there no criminal record on them?"

"That's why Murry called me from across the street. Seems the Parkers also put on private shows—live—for a rich old bastard down there. He must be a powerful old pervert— Murry said he applied the fix like it's never been laid on before. Said you'd have thought the Parker family did nothing but film Sunday school picnics after the big man's efforts in their behalf.

"Captain Murry told me it cost him a couple of damn good

vice cops. They quit the department. That's why he thought it politic to avoid the police switchboard."

"Unbelievable. But why me, Grant?"

"You ever hear of Silas Camp?"

"Sure, everybody's heard of him."

"Any reason the famous billionaire should have it in for you?"

"Hell no. I've heard of him, but I'm sure he's never heard of me," Brennan replied.

"Old Silas was the guy who arranged the cover-up for the Parkers. Now, Murry tells me, they're at his beck and call."

"Say," Brennan asked suddenly, "where are the Parkers now?"

"In the Ross County jail," the policeman replied. "Seems I arrested them just after the judges went home, so they can't make bond till morning. Gives me a little time to work up the case. And because I'm such a nice guy, I put Sandra in a foster home instead of a cell."

"Sure sounds like a blackmail plot to me," Brennan observed. "And you think Silas Camp is behind all this? Sure the Parkers aren't operating on their own?"

"Murry told me that once Old Man Camp gets his hooks into people like the Parkers, their freedom to take independent action just no longer exists.

"I'd guess Silas sends the Parkers here and there around the country pulling this same fraud, or whatever variation is appropriate, on suckers like you. They get some poor bastard all properly charged with molesting, and then old Silas can make the victim jump when he yells frog. Probably the Parkers never show up when the case comes up for trial. They're very sorry, but they're just too busy or too upset and they want to forget it all. No complaining witness so the case is dismissed. Meanwhile, Camp has got what he wanted out of the guy who was set up."

"I could hang a lot of appropriate four-letter words on the

whole damn crew." Brennan said as he ordered another round. "Is there any way I can bring charges against Camp? I'm one complaining witness that will damn sure show up for the trial. Might at least teach Camp to keep his hired help at home."

"I don't know, Doc. There should be plenty of possibilities. Suppose we confer with the state's attorney in the morning before court. I think this bunch should be kept off the streets for a while. Besides, after the job the Parkers did on Mr. Keller this morning, I think he feels just as strongly about all this as we do."

Miller laughed, then added, "You should've seen Keller's face when I walked into his office, escorting Parker, his new-found hero, all dressed up in handcuffs. You should've seen it, Doc.

"Oh—almost forgot one little detail. The Parkers also have a legitimate job. Sure, it's probably a sham, but officially they're bonified employees of Camp. They work for one of his companies, an outfit called Pembroke Drugs."

"What?" Brennan put a restraining hand on the captain's arm as he rose to leave the table.

"Do you know Pembroke Drugs, Doc?"

"Let me get this straight, Captain. You say Silas Camp owns Pembroke Drugs?"

"He sure does."

"I'll be damned." Brennan lit a cigarette and sat staring off into space.

"Okay, Doc, you better tell me about it." Miller's voice was calm, but his interest was soaring.

"Sit back, Grant, and relax. Let's have another beer. I have one hell of a postscript for your story, now that it's all fallen into place. I'm going to tell you all about good old Gastropep, and a drug company called Pembroke, and a dumb pediatrician named Patrick Brennan."

CHAPTER XIV

Friday was bright and clear and white. Sunlight poured into the packed courtroom, giving it an aura of rich warmth. This plus the subdued noise and distinctive odor of a crowd all mingled into a potpourri that satisfied the senses and unconsciously oriented those assembled toward the serious business at hand—the court hearing on aggravation and mitigation in the case of the State versus Jacqueline Teal.

The defense attorney made the initial presentation. Delaney had not been able to produce any character witnesses to testify that his client had some vestige of saving grace, some trait that would tend to alleviate the impending pronouncement of punishment. He had searched for such witnesses, but they simply did not exist. He had considered using James Teal, but rejected the idea. Too many already considered his sins to be considerably more than mere passive negligence.

Delaney dared not risk putting Jacqueline Teal on the stand in her own behalf. No telling what she might do or say. He could not even refer to his client as lady, wife, or mother. So he had to limit his presentation to skillful mouthings of the tired old platitudes—about how she was penitently throwing herself upon the mercy of the court. The lawyer could only pray that the sympathy to which he so confidently referred did, in fact, exist in the mind and heart of the judge.

Then the state's attorney took over. Captain Grant Miller testified as the investigating officer. In turn the county coroner, Dr. Karl Winston, described the condition of Helen's body. He further reviewed the evidence of chronic abuse and injury as reflected by the forensic examination of the corpse.

Next Keller called the psychiatrist to the witness stand. He felt quite sure that this witness would nail it all down. "Please state your name," Harold began.

"Myron Greenglass."

"Your occupation?"

"Physician."

"You are licensed to practice medicine in all its branches in the state of Illinois?" Keller asked.

"Yes."

"Are you a specialist in any particular field of medicine?"

"Psychiatry," Dr. Greenglass replied with pride.

"Where do you practice?"

"In Chicago. My office is located at 700 North Michigan Avenue."

"Doctor, are you affiliated with any hospitals, medical schools, or do you hold teaching—"

"Your Honor," Delaney interrupted, "the defense will be happy to recognize Dr. Greenglass as an eminent expert in the field of psychiatry. May we proceed?"

Judge Waggoner nodded his agreement.

Keller, scowling petulantly, continued his inquiry. "Did you, Dr. Greenglass, have occasion to examine Mrs. Jacqueline Teal, the defendant in this case?"

"I did. I was one of a panel of three psychiatrists who examined Mrs. Teal."

Jackie had tensed up the instant Dr. Greenglass was called to the witness stand. As Greenglass approached the subject of her sanity, her anxiety perceptibly increased. Delaney correctly guessed that she was afraid the psychiatrist was going to declare her insane.

"What did your examination of Mrs. Teal consist of?" Keller asked.

"A routine physical examination. A lengthy session with

Mrs. Teal along the line of a psychiatric evaluation. I ordered psychological tests to be administered by a competent clinical psychologist. And," he added, "I interviewed her parents. They came to see me in my Chicago office."

"What, if anything, did the psychological testing of Mrs. Teal reveal, Dr. Greenglass?"

"Objection," Delaney interjected. "Hearsay."

"Your Honor," Harold blustered, "this was a series of psychological tests performed at the direction of this court. By a—"

"Overruled," Judge Waggoner declared. "For your reason, Mr. Prosecutor. But also because in a hearing such as this, pertinent hearsay testimony is allowed. Answer the question, Dr. Greenglass."

"Yes—" After a pause, Myron Greenglass said in a subdued voice, "I'm afraid I've forgotten the question, Your Honor."

At the judge's request, the court reporter repeated Keller's question. "What, if anything, did the psychological testing of Mrs. Teal reveal, Dr. Greenglass?"

"Thank you." Greenglass paused again to organize his thoughts, then said, "She has an IQ of ninety-four, well within the average range. On the Minnesota Multiphasic Personality Inventory Test, Mrs. Teal's highest scores were in scale seven, the hysteria category, where her tendencies toward immature emotional life, repression, and somatization of psychological conflict were marked. Less dramatic but significant findings were noted in scale two, the lie category. This showed her to have strong repressive-constrictive traits."

Keller stared at his star witness, realizing that few present understood the doctor's technical jargon. But he did and the judge did. There was no jury, so why beg the question with a lengthy deciphering process? "Did you also make a personal evaluation of the defendant?"

"Yes."

"And you personally interviewed Mrs. Teal's mother and father?"

"Yes," Dr. Greenglass repeated.

"You are thoroughly acquainted with the accepted legal definitions of sanity versus insanity, is that correct?"

"Yes, Mr. Keller."

"Fine," Harold said. "Now, based on the psychological tests and your personal examinations, what is your expert opinion concerning the sanity or insanity of the defendant, Jacqueline Teal."

"She is sane," the psychiatrist unequivocally replied.

"No further questions. None at all," the state's attorney said happily.

Judge Waggoner leaned back in his huge swivel chair. "Defense?"

Tom Delaney absently twirled his pen between thumb and index finger of both hands. He shifted his gaze from the psychiatrist to Jackie Teal, who obviously wanted to tell him something. Her eyes were wide and frightened, her face very rigid. "Just a moment, Your Honor," Delaney said aloud, simultaneously leaning toward his client. "Yes?" he whispered to Jackie.

"Don't you screw it up, Delaney," she hissed. "He said I ain't crazy. Don't you spoil it."

Poor, stupid woman, Delaney thought. I could cross-examine Greenglass until the cows come home, and accomplish absolutely nothing. But that's not your twisted concern. You're more afraid of being called a nut than you are of what's going to happen to you here today. And that's not insane? Then I'm the Queen of the May.

"No questions, Your Honor," he said aloud.

"The prosecution rests," States Attorney Keller announced quickly, before Delaney or anyone else could change their minds.

160

Myron Greenglass, feeling very relieved, quickly left the room, the courthouse, and Rossdale.

There followed a brief recess, after which Judge Pieter Waggoner reconvened his hearing and called Dr. Patrick Brennan to the stand to testify at the request of the court, and with the acquiescence of the opposing attorneys.

Judge Waggoner led Brennan through a lengthy voir dire, wherein it was established that he was a physician, resided in St. Louis, Missouri, was licensed to practice medicine in all its branches in both Missouri and Illinois, and was a fully trained, qualified, and certified specialist in pediatrics. A long list of memberships in professional societies, publications in various medical journals, teaching affiliations, and medical awards were recited for the benefit of the court record.

Finally this litany came to an end, and Brennan was declared legitimate.

Some of the spectators leaned forward to get a good look at the physician. The unknown factor in the Teal case, the role of this so-called expert, was about to be unveiled.

"Judge Waggoner."

"Yes, Dr. Brennan."

"When you asked me to act as a friend of the court in this matter, you said that you would give me a carte blanche, that I would have complete freedom of action—within the limits of the law, of course."

"That's true, Doctor."

"If that carte blanche is still valid, I'd like to ask that I be allowed to testify in a narrative fashion rather than in response to questions of counsel. Later, of course, I'll attempt to answer any queries I can."

"I think that will be all right. Defense?"

"No objection."

"Prosecution?"

"Well, it's a highly irregular procedure, Your Honor." The state's attorney eyed Brennan a little uneasily. "I wish all to know that I have no idea what Dr. Brennan's testimony will be. I have had only a brief contact with the doctor, and we did not discuss his opinion of this case.

"I would also like to remind the court that the doctor is not trained in the legal intricacies—"

"No speeches now, sir," the judge snapped. "You've had your say. Now, any objections to the doctor's request?"

"No objections," muttered the red-faced state's attorney.

"Good. You may proceed, Dr. Brennan."

The physician leaned back in his chair and adjusted the microphone. "Thank you, Your Honor, gentlemen. I'll try to avoid being too technical or didactic. If I start sounding like a lecturer, I apologize in advance. Please forgive me and bear with me.

"I'm a physician that specializes in the care and treatment of infants and children. As such, I am vitally interested in all facets of the problems of children—be that an infection, a trauma, a congenital abnormality, an acquired disease, or an emotional or psychological difficulty.

"Pediatrics is also very much concerned with the growth and development of the patient. The child is a dependent organism, usually sustained, loved, and nurtured by his parents. It is also true that the child is very much at the mercy of his parents. So the relationship between the child, his parents, and his environment will have a very profound effect upon his physical and mental welfare. And I am interested in this interrelationship. Because it's my business, my life's work—because I am a pediatrician.

"Today I want to concern myself with one way in which this interrelationship of child, parent, and environment occasionally goes haywire. There are many ways this can happen, but the one I want to talk about is quite pertinent to the case at hand. It is the subject of child abuse.

"Mistreatment of children is nothing new in man's history. Genesis tells us that Abraham was quite willing to sacrifice

162

his son, Isaac, when the Lord commanded him to do so. As a matter of fact, infanticide, as well as child murder, has been linked with various forms of religious worship throughout all the many years of what we call civilization. The ancient Roman Code clearly stated that a child was his father's chattel, and that the father could do with him whatever he wished— sell him into slavery, work him, even kill him. As you all know, Rome itself is said to have been founded by two abandoned infants who were suckled by a she-wolf. Child mutilation, murder, abandonment, exploitation—all have been standards of human behavior. Remember that only a few decades ago the mills and mines depended on indentured child labor for a considerable percentage of their work force. Some called it apprenticeship. Others labeled it sweatshop slavery. Whatever you call it, the kids suffered.

"Some very prominent people throughout our land still consider corporal punishment necessary to proper child rearing. We teach this doctrine in our homes, our churches, our schools. You've all heard the old maxim, 'spare the rod and spoil the child'. Is it wrong? Is it a bad concept? Or do you believe in it? If so, are you surprised to learn that some parents find it difficult to distinguish between reasonable discipline and irrational battering?"

Brennan paused, glanced briefly at his notes, then resumed his monologue. "Your own state of Illinois, since it passed mandatory reporting laws regarding child abuse in 1965, finds that hundreds of cases are reported each year. And sadly, over this country, a lot of these reported cases have proven fatal to the victims. Consequently, even greater numbers of the next generation will suffer permanent bodily or psychic damage that will scar them for the rest of their lives.

"So the problem is neither new nor rare. But it is sad. Always very sad.

"Why does it happen? Most of you in this courtroom find the whole idea horrifying. Detestable. Unnatural. Who would

163

do such a thing to a helpless baby or an innocent child?

"Indeed, child beating is repugnant to all of us. Or is it? Isn't it really a matter of the degree of the thrashing that is important here? Is there a parent in this courtroom or anywhere else who hasn't, at one time or another, been pushed to the point of being more than ready to smack the tar out of one of his own kids?

"The answer is no. It's the normal response of a tired and eternally harassed father or mother. Something comes apart at such a time, and they feel like beating the living hell out of their little monsters. But do they carry this disciplinary action to the point of doing serious physical damage to their child? No! They do not. They stop far short of an actual vindictive attack.

"So what stops the normal parent? What puts on the brakes, so to speak, so that reasonable discipline and unreasonable abuse are seen in their proper perspective? What stays the hand of parental wrath?

"Well, I think that's really why I'm here—to examine a particular case of child murder, and to express an opinion on this case in relation to the general problem it is a part of.

"Suppose I describe a hypothetical person to you. Suppose I told you that— Wait a second. I want to make one thing very clear to the court. I am not a psychiatrist. I make no claims in that field. The defendant in this case was examined by a panel of three very competent psychiatrists, and their reports on Mrs. Teal were made available to me. They are comprehensive accounts of their professional appraisals of this woman. I have borrowed from them quite heavily.

"Now, I am about to describe a person to you." Brennan looked around the room, then shifted his eyes to Jackie Teal, who was sitting as if paralyzed on the defense side of a long table. Her face was a mask. Looking directly at her, he continued in a softer tone. "This person was born into a household full of hate. She had a loveless upbringing and was constantly oppressed. She was a servant in her own home. She was never allowed to be a child, but was forced to be a tool, a device designed solely for the gratification of her parents. Never free. Chronically unhappy.

"Unloved is the term that would best describe her whole life. She tried to find happiness for herself, but after a while she became afraid to reach out for it. She'd learned that, for her at least, it just was never really there. The people she should've been able to turn to for love or sympathy or understanding or the fulfillment of any other personal needs acted as if they owed her nothing. For her, they had a slap instead of a kiss, a sermon instead of a kind word, a demand instead of a helping hand.

"There were many directors in her life, and she owed them all respect, servitude, and eternal sublimation of self. She was a Cinderella without a fairy godmother. It was hell, with no end in sight. Consequently, she was chronically afraid.

"She reacted to this sort of life by building up a complex set of defenses. She became rigid, hostile, evasive, demanding. Emotionally unstable, trusting no one. Lonely and alone. She always was alone.

"She needed help, but she'd been programed to fear help. As a child, the ones she had logically turned to for help—her parents—rejected her. Very often physically. To ask for aid meant more pain, more hurt. So she quit asking."

Dr. Brennan now directed his eyes and remarks toward the citizens in the courtroom. "What would you people of Rossdale think of a person like that? Not very pleasant, is it—that life? You might feel sorry for her, think her unfortunate. You certainly would not envy such a person. Most of you would understand that she's sick and could profit by psychiatric therapy. Even a layman could see that she'd need a lot of help. And sympathy. And understanding. And love.

"She had all the basic human needs, but they were never

satisfied. Never! It would be a big job to treat such a person, to attempt to even partially fill the void in her life."

Brennan paused. It was very still in the courtroom. "Suppose I went on to say that this person I have just described to you killed her own child by repeatedly slamming her against the bathroom floor. That she literally smashed the life out of her own daughter.

"Then what do we hear? Sympathy? No! We hear a mob crying for more blood. Understanding? That too is drowned out by the screams for revenge. Treatment? No! We hear 'hang the bitch' instead.

"We, as society, react to the brutal injustice of this murder. How? Do we attempt to understand this tragic parody of parenthood? No. We act just as she did. We mimic the murderer—by collectively assuming the same righteous viciousness that the killer personified individually. We identify with this passion and shout for more slaughter. Why?

"The person I have just described is the defendant in this case—Mrs. Jacqueline Teal. It's not a pretty picture, is it? Well, she's not a very likable person, this Jackie Teal, but she's all those things that I mentioned. And she is a killer.

"Now I'd like to talk about the killing itself. This murder was not committed in a moment of overwhelming passion. The final assault was only one in a long series of brutal attacks on the child.

"And I am certain that if Helen Teal had survived that attack last September, she would still be undergoing continual battering. To this very day!

"Why?" Brennan looked at Grant Miller. "Why? I know this has bothered a lot of you. Jackie Teal doesn't think she did anything wrong. On the contrary, she thinks she was doing what was right, what she had to do—to and for her daughter, Helen.

"I told you this Mrs. Teal is not a very likable person." This statement aroused a confused and hostile murmuring in

166

the crowd. Jackie Teal sat staring with obvious hatred at Brennan.

"Mrs. Teal knows no remorse. She told me Wednesday that she is where she is because Helen put her there. Put her in jail and put her in this trial situation. Helen did it to her!

"And I'm telling you that she is a lot of things, Mrs. Teal is. But she is honest with herself in her belief that she did not wrong her daughter. She did what she thought was right and just in her relationship with her dead child.

"Why? Why did she hurt Helen? That's also easy. Because she felt she had to. She saw it as her duty to raise an obedient, submissive, polite, and respectful child. It was her maternal duty to do this. She could not spare the rod.

"Suppose we review that fatal morning last September. On the day of her death, two-year-old Helen wet her pants. But in the Teal household, peeing in your panties was proscribed. So the cycle was set in motion. The beating began and became more vicious as it progressed. In time the child was dead. For wetting her pants.

"You know this is ridiculous. If wetting your pants at the age of two were a capital crime, none of us would be here. If this were the case. If this were true. But it was the case in the Teal house. And it was and still is true in the mind of Jacqueline Teal.

"Now I want to ask a question. Is this a sick mind, the mind of that Teal woman? We know that, given the myopic distinction between legal sanity and legal insanity, the psychiatrists had to attest to the fact that Mrs. Teal is legally sane. She knows what is right from what is wrong. Thus she is legally of sane mind. Funny, this ability to distinguish right from wrong is at the core of the whole problem. Jacqueline Teal could and did make rigid distinctions between right and wrong. In her mind she was right, her daughter was wrong. But is this a sick mind or is this healthy?

"It certainly is a classic symptom of the obsessive-compul-

167

sive mind. Action demands and provokes a violent reaction. A two-year-old wets her panties and gets a vicious beating. She cries at inopportune moments and gets it again. She gets knocked around until it kills her. And this is as it should be, according to Jacqueline Teal. I ask you again, is this sick?

"Let's look at it some more. We are talking about adults who abuse children. In this instance the attacker was the mother. It may be a father, a relative, a babysitter, or a stranger. But here it was a mother. So let's talk briefly about mothers. Normal mothers

"What do mothers do? That's easy—they mother. And that involves many things, all of which can be separated into two categories. First, there are the mechanical activities— mothers feed, clean, protect, and teach their offspring. All animals do this, but it is even more mandatory in the human than in other species because of our prolonged period of help-lessness and dependence. And if this mothering ceases, we end up with a neglected child—dirty, sick, malnourished, even starved. Unfortunately, this happens all too often.

"Now, the other category of maternal duty is what I call just plain mothering. This is one of the things that sets us above the other animals. This awareness of the importance of your offspring as an individual is not totally absent in other species, but it is essential to humans. It means tenderness and tears and comfort. It means warmth. A soft breast to climb up to when you're very little and much afraid. Or when you need protection—or think you need it. It means being held close and hugged and kissed. It means love.

"This is what little Jackie never had, and this is what Jacqueline Teal, the mother, couldn't provide. She had yearned for it as a child, but she never received it. She never under-stood what it was all about. So she feared it—much as you people in Rossdale fear her—because she simply did not understand it.

"Monica Teal, the older girl, was a very placid child. Undemanding. Obedient. A perfect baby. All she did was eat and sleep. In time, she evolved into a good servant. The mechanical mothering was sufficient to sustain Monica. She survived.

"Soon Jackie was expecting her second child. She told me she looked forward to Helen's birth during that pregnancy. She didn't know why, but I do. It was because Jacqueline realized, had in fact always known, that she was incomplete. Unfulfilled. Her own parents were unapproachable, godlike figures. Her husband could not provide what she lacked. She had no friends—she was too remote and withdrawn, and too easily aroused to violent anger. Who could like her? Who could love her? Her first child was a cipher. But the second child offered her a reprieve, one more chance at all the things she vaguely knew she lacked.

"So along came Helen, who was to provide all that Jackie had missed in life. The infant was going to mother the mother. The parent would become dependent and demanding and expect fulfillment and love from the child. A complete reversal of roles, in other words.

"Helen could not provide all these things to her mother. No infant can. So the mother was sorely disappointed once again. She remained insecure and unloved and even more frustrated.

"Helen was not like her sister. She demanded more than a mechanical mother. She demanded a complete mother. But this she just didn't have. So Helen fretted and fussed and cried and was a colicky baby.

The mother couldn't stand it. This baby was supposed to reassure her—and just look at it. Jackie was supposed to be comforted and mothered. Jackie was supposed to demand. And she did demand. For two years she demanded. She demanded things that her daughter simply could not give her, things she could not do. Consequently, and quite often, this bad baby had to be punished.

"Then, one day last September, Helen did it again. She was bad again. She wet her pants. She had to be whipped. Her mother demanded that she be potty trained at a very early age. It was the mother's right to demand, and it was the infant's duty to be obedient and submissive. To be a 'good' girl. To do what her mother wanted.

"But that day last September, Helen was a bad girl. She wet her pants. And it killed her.

"Now we already know that Mrs. Teal has a legally sane mind. About that the law is very narrow and very specific—hers is a sane mind. But is this a healthy mind? Or is it sick?"

Brennan paused to allow his audience to consider the questions he had posed. There was no whispering, no shuffling of feet. Finally Brennan turned to the judge and apologized for preaching at such length.

Judge Waggoner nodded. "Quite all right, Doctor. It's a complex problem and we need to understand it. Please continue."

"Thank you, Your Honor, but I've about said it all."

"Well then, shall we start the questions?"

Both attorneys and the judge plied Brennan with questions, most of which were intended to clarify certain aspects of the defendant's personality. Dr. Brennan again stressed the fact that Mrs. Teal was raised according to the same code of rigid discipline that she carried over into her own household. He stated that while Mrs. Teal was obviously a physical and mental adult, she was still in many respects an emotional infant.

No, Patrick Brennan did not feel that James Teal was without guilt. True, he was not the attacker in the Teal house, but he tolerated, to say the very least, the longstanding and irrational abuse that eventually resulted in Helen's death. James said he wanted no spoiled brats, and Jackie made sure his wishes were honored. Further, Brennan thought that Mr.

Teal's final rejection and desertion of his family was the last straw, that it sealed the doom of the now dead child.

Judge Waggoner asked if Dr. Brennan thought treatment— if it could be provided—would be of any benefit to Mrs. Teal.

"That's a good question, Judge. As I've said before, I firmly believe that Mrs. Teal has absolutely no feelings of guilt or remorse about the killing. I'm sure she really believes that what she did was right, and that the death was an accidental by-product of her own innate rightness. She does feel regret, for had there been no death, she would not be in jail or here in this courtroom. But that's not the same as remorse.

"Now, we know these abusing parents have a good chance if they can get intensive therapy in a favorable environment. The process requires a lot of time and attention. The therapist must provide the parent with some means of fulfilling her basic human needs so she will no longer turn to the infant for fulfillment.

"This is a long, drawn-out therapeutic program, but it's the only treatment I know of that has helped an appreciable number of patients in this particular category. The Denver group, the one that pioneered this whole study of child abuse, reports successful results in the vast majority of their cases. The failures usually involve the psychotic child beater, the sociopath, the sadist, or those who for some reason cannot be treated—often because they're caught up in a criminal situation, such as in this case, where the issue before the court is not treatment but punishment.

"I have provided you with an oversimplification of a very complex problem, Your Honor. For example, in the nonfatal case, a great deal of thought must be given to the safety of the child while the parent is undergoing therapy. A sick person, such as an abusive parent, needs help, but the potentially explosive nature of the situation must be taken into account. The child involved has a right to be safe—to live.

"The nonfatal case usually ends up in a juvenile court. If

necessary, the safety of the children can be assured by making them wards of the court—perhaps taking them away from the parents and putting them in a foster home, at least temporarily. And, as you well know, Your Honor, this removal gives a judge a powerful means of insuring that abusive parents get the therapy they need. All he need say is that if they want to have their children back, they must continue in the treatment program until the therapists feel they are capable of handling that responsibility. And until they can provide a reasonably safe environment for the little ones.

"Unfortunately, that is not the issue in this case. Helen is already dead. So this type of program won't help her. But Monica is still alive. And Mrs. Teal is young enough to have more children. I've seen many cases where subsequent children just started the whole cycle of abuse all over again.

"Now I have said that I think Mrs. Teal has a sick mind. Her sickness should be treated. She could be helped.

"But this is not a hospital or a physician's clinic or a juvenile court. This is a criminal court. Here, Mrs. Teal represents the epitome of felonies—murder. You'll notice I've tried to stay away from the legal implications of that fact. Call it cowardice or deviousness or whatever you like. I readily admit to stressing what I know—medicine—at the expense of what the law says you, Your Honor, must do in regard to this defendant. You didn't ask me to come here to play lawyer, but to testify within the limits of my professional qualifications.

"I'd just like to say this much more. I know that the laws of this land are not therapeutically oriented. They're punishment oriented. They clearly state that infanticide is murder, and this is surely true. They further set guidelines that the court must follow when dispensing justice in these cases.

"There's a lot of talk about treatment and rehabilitation within our penal system. But the truth is that neither the law nor the penal system is therapeutically oriented. The high percentage of parolees who return to crime as soon as they get the chance attests eloquently to the fact that these prisoners had no effective treatment while they were incarcerated. Rather, the major theme was punishment.

"What has all this to do with Jacqueline Teal? Potentially a great deal. I've said I believe she could be treated. I can also predict that she would almost certainly respond favorably to the proper treatment.

"However, the law says she must go to prison for her crime. And what's she likely to get in prison? The penal philosophy involves a removal of one's identity of self, so she will become one of many anonymous prisoners. No name, just a number. Her life will be orderly, disciplined, and dull. She will be surrounded by rigid symbols of authority. And they will control her every move every moment of the day and night. Her existence will become a series of responses to commands. She will have to be quiet and obedient.

"In other words, Your Honor, prison will simply be a harsher version of all the things that contributed to Mrs. Teal's becoming a murderess in the first place. As Dr. Kempe said, 'punishment is the genesis of the disease.'

"How will Mrs. Teal respond to this environment? I think it safe to say that she will simply get worse."

Brennan turned to face the judge. "That is not a very pleasant prospect. Not pleasant for Jacqueline Teal. Not pleasant for Judge Waggoner. It puts both of you in the same unfortunate circumstance. She is a victim of her life. And you, Your Honor, are a victim of the law.

"I don't envy you your duty, Judge. Not at all. I can see the problems you face in this case, and I feel sorry for you. Sorry that the law will require you to do what I strongly suspect you believe to be wrong." Brennan shifted his gaze to Jacqueline Teal. "Because if society dictates imprisonment for this woman, you, Your Honor, will have to make sure that her sentence extends through and beyond all her remaining childbearing years. You know that imprisonment will feed the sickness that has already resulted in the murder of one child, so you will have to make sure that Jacqueline Teal will not have another child after she's released."

"Dr. Brennan," the state's attorney interrupted.

"Yes?"

"Am I to understand that you're making a plea for probation? If so, let me remind you that the laws of Illinois fortunately do not provide for probation in a capital case."

"I object to this interruption, Your Honor," Delaney interjected.

"Overruled!" Judge Waggoner turned toward Brennan and said in a softer voice, "I think the doctor would be quite happy to answer Mr. Keller's question. Dr. Brennan?"

"Gladly, Your Honor," Brennan replied. "If you recall, Mr. Keller, I was answering the judge's question about the potential effects of treatment on a person I consider to be very sick—Mrs. Teal. I was interpreting her medical prognosis in view of the circumstances that had to be considered if my answer was to have any meaning to the court.

"You asked about probation. That's a legal matter. I was talking about therapy—and that, sir, is a medical matter. But how do you separate the effects of one discipline from those of the other? Logically, we should not have to make this distinction. A mentally sick individual should receive proper treatment, whenever possible. But in this case the law says that shall not happen.

"Who is at fault in this case, Mr. Prosecutor? Certainly Jacqueline Teal is. But is she the only one? Is it any longer excusable to just say it's too bad we haven't evolved to the point of being able to provide basic moral justice to a sick human being? And let it go at that? I say no. I submit to you that in this case the law is wrong. Pathetically, inexcusably inadequate.

"I've said the law is penalty oriented in this instance. Why?

174

Because you people made it so. You—you people of Rossdale.

"You have shown me during this past week that you want to penalize. That you want your eye for an eye.

" 'Vengeance is mine, sayeth the Lord.' Mine too, sayeth the citizens of Rossdale. This is certainly not limited to Rossdale, but here, the will of society has recently come very close to becoming the will of a mob ready to extract its pound of flesh.

"But these crises passed. So society now unloads the responsibility of meeting its demands for retribution on the shoulders of Judge Waggoner.

"Those who are most vindictive rationalize away their sanctimonious vengefulness by saying that all felons are the same. You can't cure them so lock 'em up. These same people are quick to point out that human nature never changes. But human knowledge does change. So why doesn't society change accordingly?

"Maybe someday our laws will recognize the fact that effective treatment promises rehabilitation, a return to society as a productive member for many, many sick people whose illnesses cause them to violate the standards of behavior necessary to maintaining our society. Maybe someday this will happen in our land. Unfortunately, that day is not yet here."

The doctor sat back, exhausted. "No, Judge, I don't envy you. But I have to admire you. Rarely have I encountered such courage as you have demonstrated by letting me have my say here today. And if there are no other rewards, Your Honor, rest assured that you have at least earned my heartfelt thanks and humble respect."

"Jacqueline Teal." The voice was firm, full of dignity, but the face seemed to have taken on great age. "Jacqueline Teal, it is the sentence of this court that you be —"

Dr. Brennan closed the heavy door. He had heard enough.

He walked slowly, yet purposefully, out of the place of justice.

It was time to leave Rossdale. His work was finished. Or was it? His own idea of justice seemed to have become somewhat confused. The Parkers and, maybe in a minute way, even McNeill and Silas Camp—they were all going to have to make retribution for their offenses against him. And this was right, he thought. Yet, it was somehow different when society demanded similar retribution from Jacqueline Teal.

He had rejoiced at the prospect of those who had wronged him receiving the full blast of society's wrath. Yet he wondered if this perhaps indicated a latent kinship with those he had so recently criticized for their vindictiveness. "Physician, heal thyself," seemed to be very applicable advice right now.

Maybe the Parkers were sick, maybe Camp was. None of it quite seemed to escape at least a hint of illness, not even justice itself.

Was this the final diagnosis then? Almost universal illness. So what? What was he—anyone—prepared to do about it? Still, there could be a cure. That's what made him so damn mad. No one even seemed to care.